WITH TIES THAT BIND

WITH TIES THAT BIND

Broken Bonds, Book One

TRISHA WOLFE

Interior Design and Formatting by:

www.emtippettsbookdesigns.com

"There is always some madness in love. But there is also always some reason in madness."

~Friedrich Nietzsche

CHAPTER 1

THREE DAYS AFTER RESCUE

AVERY

Rocking.

I can still feel the rocking.

I come awake at night to the pitch black—to the void of space and time and consciousness, but always the rocking. As if I'm still trapped in the belly of that boat. Panic grips me so acutely, I thrash and scream until the hospital room comes into focus.

Even then, it's not the reassurance of my surroundings that quiets my hell and stops the screams. I held them in for so long, never giving that monster what he most desired, and now they pour out; a flood channeled through me. Like the dam holding them back cracked with the first one, and my sanity—the mending glue—dissolved under the swell.

But then I feel his hand in mine. That's what brings me

back from the brink of madness. I suck in a shuddering breath and let the shiver subside before I look over at him.

Quinn sleeps upright in the chair with his coat bunched up underneath his head. His arm rests on my bed, his hand clutched to mine. My screams never wake him, and I wonder if it's all in my head—if I might still be inside a nightmare that I can't wake from.

He could be a delusion. Some kind of sick dream within the nightmare that offers a glimpse of peace before I'm swallowed by the darkness all over again. Because the screams that blister my throat as they claw up from the sickness…no one could sleep through.

Only he does, and he's been here every night since I shed my first tear, embarrassed that I feared being left alone in the hospital room.

I ease closer to him, lacing my fingers through his. His scent of leather and cologne—so much like a cop—settles over me. I inhale deeply, accepting this moment of peace. Just knowing he's here.

When I'm released tomorrow, what then? When the silence of my own home mocks me and the emptiness consumes my life, how will I cope? I've never feared being alone before.

I don't know how to be a victim.

What's more, I don't want to fear that monster. He's dead. I saw him dead with my own eyes. But there's still this twisting nausea in the pit of my stomach. The darkness whispering that my tormentor lurks everywhere I look. Can a person die of fear? Some nights it feels as if my heart will burst, and I'm tempted to let the panic finally consume me.

Quinn stirs and I release his hand, scared that if he wakes, he'll be the first to let go.

A low knock travels through the room, causing another scream to fire from my lungs. A figure stands in the open doorway, and I know it's Simon… That fucking sick fuck is still alive.

"Avery, it's okay." Sadie enters the room, her voice soft and her face catching the dim glow of the monitor.

"Oh, my God." I press my hand to my chest, shame sweeping over me. "I just… Sometimes it's hard when I first wake up."

"I know," she says. Her gaze shifts from me to Quinn before she settles on the edge of the bed. "I still wake up screaming some nights."

Anger burns lava-red in my vision, my chest aflame. I don't understand whom I'm angry with...or why…but hearing that all this time—all these *years*—hasn't changed anything for Sadie, makes me want to lash out.

"Why are you here?" I ask, the venom thick in my voice. Immediately, regret douses the flames. God, it's a never-ending cycle. "I'm sorry…"

"Don't be." She stands and extends her hand. "You're going to need that anger."

Confusion pushes my brows together, but I accept her hand. "For what?"

With her help, I climb out of the bed, my body—every muscle and bone—sore from the days of torture inflicted on me. As she guides me toward the hallway, I glance back at Quinn.

"He's fine. Can sleep through a hurricane," she assures. "I tried to wake him up once when he fell asleep at his desk"—she shakes her head slowly—"dead to the world."

"Maybe that's why he drew the short straw to be the one to sit with me." I take a seat on the waiting bench. "He's the only one who can get a full night despite my fits." I try to smile, but the deep cut running through my bottom lip stings from the effort.

Sadie's silence draws my gaze up to her. A serious expression tugs her mouth into a grim line. "Quinn's here on his own. I had no idea," she says.

I look down at my lap, the hospital bracelet circling my wrist. I twirl it, my thoughts muddled. "Then why—?"

"You'll have to ask him." She sits down beside me. "I've come for an entirely different reason. I'm not here to comfort you, Avery. I'm not going to tell you lies about how therapy will help, about how time will heal you. That all you need to do is be strong and fight your demons."

"Damn," I say, a breathy laugh escaping. "Don't sugarcoat it."

"I won't." Her eyes lock with mine; hers unblinking and lit with a surreal gleam that chills me to my bones. "We only discuss this once. From here on out, no matter what you decide, it stays here. Between us."

I should be terrified. This is not the Sadie I know. The woman sitting before me now is cold and methodical, and what she whispers to me in the dark corridor of the hospital should send me fleeing in horror. But as she continues, telling me about a man sitting at a bar, her plan for this man…an eerie calm envelops me, soothing away any trace of fear. Her voice drifts to me, lulling me into a welcome camaraderie, and for the first time since I was plucked from the hellish bowels of The Countess, I feel as if I can take a breath without fearing my own screams.

I make the pact.

It's as simple as slicing open a dead body…which I've done many times over. Then all the fear, the panic, the screams—it all ends. That is the control over my life Sadie grants me in this moment, and I cling to it like a life raft. I crave it so deeply, I'm willing to sell my soul for it.

And so I do.

When I climb back into the hospital bed, I'm no longer the same woman Quinn hauled from that dungeon. I'm not fixed; far from it. But I feel stronger. Only as I go to lay my hand in his…I halt.

Quinn can never know.

Sadie's warning is more than common sense; it's a test.

One that I'm bound to fail if I let myself fall for the detective who's held my hand through the screams and sheltered me from the dark. All done in secrecy, because these are not things done in the light, where we must own to our desires.

So now I have a secret, too. I slip my hand into his large, rough one and curl up next to his strong arm, savoring the feel of his comfort for the last time.

CHAPTER 2

GAME CHANGER

DETECTIVE ETHAN QUINN

Arlington, Virginia is on the map.

And not in a good way. Not that it wasn't already well known—what, with the National Cemetery and the Pentagon, and DC right across the river. But it's always been a peaceful sort of city. A short drive for politicians and other DC types alike to escape to.

It won't ever be the same.

My city is a blister, an eyesore, a blemish on the face of the country. Even after nearly a month, social media is still buzzing with reports of the serial killings. There's even a hashtag for the Arlington Slasher. A dead serial killer has his own fucking hashtag.

What the hell.

Every day that I walk through the ACPD doors, I try to put the case behind me. It's time to move on, but that blister just keeps eating away. It's a festering pus pocket of self-loathing right in the pit of my stomach.

I pop an antacid, chewing on my right side. I'm still not used to the gap from my missing—*stolen*—tooth. Fuck Simon Whitmore. AKA the *Arlington Slasher*. AKA the *Blood Count*. I can't believe a damn lab geek got the better of me. How the hell did a demented twist like Simon elude us for as long as he did?

Simon's own words stated he was an apprentice to Lyle Connelly—a person of interest in one of the first cases Sadie and I worked together—and it's possible Simon learned a thing or two from his master. But without me having any access to Connelly himself, having to trust in Sadie's profile, I'm not sure I'll ever be able to accept this outcome. It's just that all the pieces don't align. And I need the puzzle neat and exact to let it rest for good.

But it won't ever match up. And one of the main reasons for that?

Me.

If I start to dig, if I try to unearth the whole truth, I have to come clean about my role.

We all did what we had to in order to rescue Avery Johnson. Even me. I made a bargain with myself the night I followed Sadie to the memorial. I knew the consequences. I looked them square in the eye and told them to fuck off.

I made the right call. At least, I made the call I had to in order to protect Sadie—to look out for my partner.

Christ. I drag my hands down my face, resting my elbows on my desk, and stare at the whiteboard along my office wall. Across from me, images of a recent, brutal attack are strung on the board. A woman's face beaten so badly, we couldn't even run facial recognition on her.

It's like the spree killings opened Pandora's box and unleashed a swarm of demented chaos on Arlington. Once the gates of hell were thrown wide, it invited every sick perp to march straight in, trying to one-up the gruesome murders.

I swear, there's some underground club where these twisted fucks collaborate. A bunch of psychopaths just hanging around, deciding where to strike next.

And Arlington is now on the map.

From my peripheral, I glimpse a jean jacket. Against my will, my neck directs my head to swivel, my eyes growing wide as I wait to make out Sadie's petite form. But just as quickly, I remember she's not here.

My gaze follows one of the analysts as she heads through the bullpen, her hips swinging. She's not Sadie. She's not my partner.

It's late. My brain is overworked. I should leave, but the only place I want to go is no longer an option. I don't have an excuse to visit Avery anymore. As screwed up as it is, I've never slept as sound as I did the nights I spent watching over her in the hospital room.

Am I a sick shit for wishing she knew I was there? For wanting her to need me still? She seems to have recovered at an alarming speed, picking up at work like she was never abducted by one of her own assistants. Yeah, Avery needs me about as much as Sadie does. I should get a hobby. Or a pet.

Fuck.

I start to pack up my laptop when a blonde coasts past my door. *Avery.*

I fumble through my case files, searching for anything on the newest case to give me a reason to go after her. I come up with nothing. I slump back in my chair and glance up. The blonde is talking to Carson—and she's not Avery. But my dick hasn't caught up to that realization yet, and he twitches in my slacks. Annoyed, I close my eyes, and despite all conscious effort, a clear visual of the last time I saw Avery springs to mind.

Her hands tucked into the back pockets of her jeans…lab coat opening up in front to reveal her white T-shirt stretched tightly across her chest. The perfect swell of her breasts… nipples hardening…

Shit. My fucking cock is rock-fucking-hard and throbbing. I'm a damn glutton for punishment, that's the truth of it. Not only that, I'm no better than the sick bastards I put away. Thinking of my colleague like that. Especially after all she's been through.

The last thing she needs is some hard-leg detective

hanging around, drooling all over her COD reports like a fucking dipshit.

It didn't used to be this way. I'm not sure when it changed, but it did. Maybe it was the night I followed Sadie to The Lair. Seeing my partner going into a forbidden, deviant environment and imagining what she was doing—or letting be done to *her*—on the inside.

The imagination is a hell of a thing.

Ever since then, my head's been a mess. I knew Sadie had a past. I knew she was tortured because of it. And I damn sure knew she wasn't as innocent as she tried to appear. But hell—a BDSM club?

And when she showed up to my crime scene in that dress… *Motherfucker*. I've never been so close to breaking my code of honor before. But my conviction for maintaining respect for my partner won out.

However, a man can only be tested so many times before he breaks.

And Avery Johnson is a whole different kind of temptation.

The line drawn between us isn't as distinct. It's blurred just enough that I could easily cross right over—but I don't like blurry boundaries. It's a trap that will have my balls in an ethical vise if I don't get my shit together.

Where I was able to draw a don't-fucking-cross-line with Sadie, it seems I just can't help myself when it comes to the hot little medical examiner. Every time she's in my office, I wage a war within myself. One side of me recalling the bruises and cuts, the pain she suffered at the hands of a serial killer, and all I want to do is protect her. Hold her hand again in the still, dark quiet of our own making and keep her safe.

But then there's a degenerate side of me that fantasizes about throwing her across my desk, spreading her creamy thighs wide. Pushing her underwear aside, lowering my zipper, and driving in hard and deep, while her brown eyes devour me.

My cock jumps, and I feel a spurt of pre-cum shoot along my leg. With a thick groan, I twist my chair around and adjust the neglected, aching member of my body.

Truth is, it might not even be my attraction for Avery that's got me this bad off. I know it's wrong. I know that fine line shouldn't be crossed. But this past case crept into all of us. Even me. Twisting me and revealing a debased side that I've only ever believed existed in the "bad guy."

Once you lower the barrier just enough to allow that deviancy past your armor, it taints you. You can dance with evil, telling yourself you're in control—that you'll only use it to crack the case. But the truth is, that darkness leaves a stain. You don't use it.

It uses you.

Or maybe it's always been there, harboring on the edge, waiting for me to let it in.

Fuck that.

I push these disastrous thoughts aside with a deep, cleansing breath. I'm tired. I'm exhausted. The only nights I've been able to sleep a full six hours since I saw Avery chained up in the hull of that boat were the nights I spent with her in the hospital.

Even now, there are times that I can't look at Avery without seeing the bruises that once marred her pretty face. The cut that tore through her bottom lip. We got the guy, yeah. He can never hurt her again. So why can't I move on to the next case?

And all this shit in my head…it's pretty simple. I haven't been with a woman since Jenna left. That was almost four months ago. My wife—soon to be *ex*-wife—decided she couldn't stand being married to a cop anymore. And even before then, it had been a while since we fucked. Damn, a while doesn't quite stress the full year I've spent hard-up and sex depraved.

Having to keep my head in the game during the chase for the killer got me through the roughest part, but I'm damn near ready to find any piece of ass and bury my cock just to get some relief.

You can't fault a guy there. Maybe it would clear my head, and by the time Sadie returns from her *vacation*, all these inappropriate thoughts will stop. They need to *stop*.

It's either that, or transfer out of the department.

That thought sobers me right up. It's been a gnawing consideration since the conversation I had with Sadie in the hospital. That's the night I sold my soul. For Sadie, for my partner, I'd do it again. Not just because of the annoying attraction to her—fuck that. I'm a pig, but I'm not a complete asshole. I care about her, but as a member of my team and because she's my partner. And that's why I did what I had to do. I looked the other way. It was the first time in my life that the right choice wasn't written out in bold font.

So I chose to do nothing.

Even now, it's a complicated mix of emotions that I'm not at all comfortable exploring, and it's why I can't stand the sight of myself in the mirror. For the first time in my whole career, I went outside the law.

For that, I should transfer Sadie or myself to another department.

But there's also a reason why I can't let that happen, either. The detective in me needs to keep her close, observe her. Investigate. I told her that I didn't want to know—and on some level, I still don't—but that won't stop me from seeking the truth.

It's what I do. Who I am. Turning a blind eye to her involvement in the murder of Lyle Connelly momentarily stripped me of my own damn identity. Some days, I'm sure the only way to get that back is by uncovering everything.

Simon may've taken the wrap for Connelly's murder, but with both Simon and Connelly dead, and no one left to interrogate, one very big question remains: who covered up for Sadie? And the even bigger one: why?

Regardless if the case is closed, everyone involved with it satisfied with the neat way it was wrapped up, I know these burning questions will eventually tear through our partnership. Only, what the fuck will I do with that truth once I have it?

I'm right back to that festering pus pocket, but of a different nature. The kind that will eat me alive if I ever let anything bad happen to Sadie.

It's a fucking vicious cycle.

A knock sounds at my door. Shoving the sickening thoughts down farther into that twisting pit, I look up from my desk. "Yeah?"

Carson peeks his head inside. "Detective Quinn, you have a call."

My brow furrows. "Why the hell didn't they call my cell if they wanted me?"

Carson shrugs, but the concern on his face already tells me something's wrong. "It's Avery. She sounds…drunk."

He has my undivided attention. "Shut the door."

His head jerks back, surprise registering on his boyish features for a brief second before he does as ordered. At the soft *click*, I stretch out my arms and crack my knuckles. Crick my neck to the side, preparing myself to take this call.

Deliberately checking my emotions, I clear my throat and pick up the phone. "Avery."

A blast of loud music greets my ear, followed by shouts

crackling into the line. "Quinn! Can you hear me?"

My fingers curl tight around the receiver. "Where are you?"

A pause where more music bleeds through the line, then: "Somewhere. A bar. I think..." A pause. "I might need a ride," she slurs, stretching out the last word awkwardly.

"Why didn't you call Sadie?" I squeeze my eyes closed at my condescending tone. As if both Avery and Sadie have some inseparable bond that now unites them as victimized women. That's not what I meant to imply.

I go to correct myself when she blurts, "I'm sooo horny. Cooome get me."

Jesus H. Christ. I set the phone on the desk for a second so I can collect myself. Running my hands down my face, I stare at the whiteboard again. I no longer understand what is happening in my department...if I ever did. It's possible I've been wearing blinders this whole time. The separation with Jenna causing me to overlook obvious disparities within my own ranks.

When did my eyes open?

Resigned, I grab the phone. "Stay put. Don't you dare go anywhere with *any*one until I get there." I hang up before she can retaliate—before she can destroy the very necessary wall I've erected between my co-workers and myself.

I don't think, I don't try to rationalize anymore—I grab the pen and sign the divorce papers on my desk. Then clutch my keys and blazer, checking my shoulder strap and gun once, before I head out of my office.

I slap the packet against Carson's chest as I pass. "Put that in the mail for me." Carson gives me an inquisitive look, but I keep going. Not looking back.

At least there are some small mercies. Avery called *me*. Not Carson. Which means I'm neutral in her book. There's some shred of rational thought in her brain despite the amount of alcohol fueling her poor judgment, and somehow, she knew to call safe, guarded, neutral Quinn.

That's me. A genuine hero to young, drunk women everywhere.

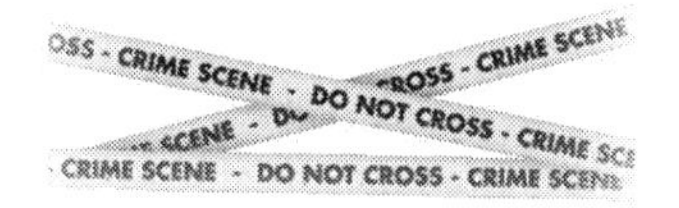

The bar I track Avery to is a real dive. On my way here, I had one of the techs ping Avery's call to my phone, praying that I wouldn't find myself pulling into The Lair. I doubt I could handle that right now—walking in to see Sadie and Reed performing some kinky rope show.

I let that very festering thought fade into the background of my mind as I enter Hooligans, which is a damn good name for this shithole.

Five-some-odd rowdy college guys surround a visibly sloshed Avery. They throw back shots, encouraging her to do the same. She's just about to tip one to her mouth as I approach and swipe it from her hand.

"Hey—" Her glassy eyes zero in on my face and she squints, then recognition hits. The depth of their brown startles me. "Quinn. You guys…this is Quinn. The detective I was telling you about."

The sudden shift in mood is immediate. The announcement of a "cop" never goes over well with partying college kids. Which begs the fucking question: just what the hell is a respectable medical examiner doing hanging out with a bunch of pricks?

"Hey, man." One of them nods my way. "Want a shot?"

I scowl. "I'm on the clock."

"Fucking bummer, dude." He takes a long pull off his bottleneck, then cocks his head. "But she's not, right? So let the lady have some fun."

Balls of steel on this one. He's either bolstered by alcohol, or he's just another entitled shit. I fucking hate kids.

Shifting my blazer, I brace my fists on my hips, flashing him *my* steel. His gaze goes right to my GLOCK and he shrugs, backing up to order a shot.

"Avery, it's time to go." I reach for her just as she ducks away.

"One more drink…" The strap of her barely there, skintight tank slips down her shoulder as she turns toward the bar top to flag the bartender.

Tamping down the fierce need to right it, I grip the edge of the counter near her waist. I'm completely out of my element, and I hate it. Give me a good perp with an assignment, and I'm your man. Babysitting drunken medical examiners who've recently been abducted and tortured…and I know shit-all how to handle the situation.

This is obvious as Avery whirls around and whoops when a bass-filled song blasts over the sound system. I stand beside her, an awkward cop statue, as she lifts her hands in the air and tosses her head back and forth. Her blond hair whips my chest as she undulates closer, rolling her hips provocatively. I suck in a sharp breath at the feel of her ass grinding up against my cock.

I need to leave. *Now.*

"All right. Fun time's over," I say, this time grabbing her wrists and tugging her out of the group of guys. The collective discontent of their "boos" sets my jaw.

Avery twists out of my hold and is heading back into the fray before I can stop her. I watch, dumbfounded, as she wriggles her way on top of the counter and pushes herself up to stand. "You want it?" she hollers.

College boys all over get a glimpse of their wet dreams as Avery sways her hips, roaming her hands up her thighs and over her breasts. She pulls her tank up, showing off a trim, tan belly with a silver chain linked around her midsection.

Against my will, my own damn hard-on makes an appearance—but I check myself quickly. *Not now, buddy.*

You're not getting a say.

Sure, I have my twisted issues, and I'm not blind. Jenna always accused me of being clueless to anything outside of work, but I'm still human. Avery has it…in all the right places. But I'd be a creep to get a thrill out of this display.

That thought smacks me hard with a dose of hypocrisy. Just minutes ago, I was fantasizing about her—not for the first time—and thinking real hard about finding *anyone* to break my year of celibacy.

No matter how badly I'd love for Avery to be that anyone, I'd never act on it. You don't mix work and pleasure. Ever. Look but don't touch. Fantasize, but don't initiate. I'm just doomed to be tortured by the hot trim in my department. That's my punishment.

Regardless, I won't let Avery do something she'll regret when she sobers up. I know she's suffering. I get that she's probably going through a hell of a lot more torturous thoughts than me, and she's only trying to figure out how to deal. I completely understand all that psychobabble.

But not here. Not now. Not on my watch.

I push my way through the suddenly swarming crowd of testosterone circling Avery below and reach up toward her. "Come on, Avery. Let me help you down."

"There better be a dollar in that hand, Quinn. I think you need this more than anyone." As she turns, rolling her hips suggestively, she reaches into her pocket and produces a baggie.

My internal siren goes off, loud and flashing. Hiking myself up on a barstool, I snatch the bag and look around the bar. "Who gave her this shit?"

Blank stares, like frat boys caught in headlights, glare back at me.

"It's hers, man," balls of steel speaks up. "She's been popping since she got here."

Dammit. This isn't good. Not at all. I'm way, way out of my depth. Sadie should be the one here—she'd know how to help Avery. I sniff the baggie, getting a whiff of something chemical-like. A kind of cut cocaine smell, but I can tell by the texture that's not what it is.

Before the thought even enters my mind to bring her in, I'm decided. Her ass is going home. Today's not the day to start flying straight by arresting renowned medical examiners.

I pocket the baggie, then scoop Avery's legs, depositing her over my shoulder. Her feet flail as I march her out of the bar, her fists banging against my back. I click my car alarm off and open the door, dropping her down onto the passenger-seat.

"You're a buzz kill, you know that?" she slurs. But just the same, she reaches for her seatbelt and attempts to fasten herself in.

With a grunt, I lean over her and click it into place. "If you have to yack, try to announce it first."

As I slip into my seat, I grip the steering wheel, trying to figure out how we got here. How the hell did we get to this point?

Avery rests her cheek against the seat, her dark eyes assessing me through a haze of alcohol. "Sadie was right. Your gray streaks are distinguished and sexy."

This raises my eyebrows. And like the sick glutton that I am, I probe. "Sadie said that, huh? Doesn't sound like the profiler I know."

"*Pfft*." Avery waves off my comment. "You don't know her one…little…bit."

It pains me how accurate that statement is, even coming from a drunk Avery. "Really," I say, cranking the car and pulling onto the street. "Then why don't you enlighten me."

A sudden silence falls between us. I peek over as Avery fiddles with her seatbelt, her demeanor antsy. "Avery, you can confide in me. If there's something…"

"There's not," she snaps. She sniffs hard, shaking her head as if to clear it. "Forget I said anything. I'm drunk. I'm fucked up, Quinn. I don't know what I'm saying."

I flip the blinker and turn onto her road. Once we're parked in her driveway, I rest my wrists on the steering wheel and stare at the dark little house, my thoughts roaring in the quiet of the car. "You're not fucked up, Aves. You're human. We all have to be a little unhinged to work the kind of job we do." I glance at her, my eyes drawn to the scar running diagonally along her lip. "And you've suffered this job more than most. It's just going to take…time. Time to feel like yourself again."

She blinks a couple of times, then tosses her head, flipping her blond hair off her shoulder. "He should've killed me. Because whatever part he left alive, whatever he didn't succeed in stealing…is dead anyway."

A pain swells to life in the center of my chest. When we rescued Avery, somehow, I imagined the story would end. That was completely ignorant of me, I know. Maybe even a bit arrogant. With all I've seen, every evil I've witnessed, I know better. But just once, I wanted a happy ending.

This is the harsh, unvarnished truth of our reality, though. The story goes on, and Avery must struggle through it. I'm just not equipped to be the person she needs—the hero to help her reach the other side of that struggle.

Even if that nagging pain in my chest is contradicting me with a resounding: I *want* to be.

As if she suspects what I'm thinking, Avery reaches over and grabs ahold of my blazer. Pulling herself over the console, I allow her to haul me closer, and she stops a hair's breadth away from my face.

"You're not as tough as you think, Quinn." Her gaze flicks over my face, intently tracing my features. "I could ride you like a rodeo cowgirl and lasso your cock with the sweetest pussy you've ever felt…I'd even let you handcuff me so you'd feel in control…"

Jesus Christ. The air in the car freezes. I try not to breathe, to make a sound, as I focus on controlling the deviant member of my body that—with every fucking fiber of my being—wants to lay claim to her proposition.

Reining in my hormones, I look at Avery—really *see* her. The pain she's trying her damndest to disguise. That leashes my desire real quick.

"Sleep it off, Avery," I say, wrenching her hands from my blazer.

Anger splashes her cheeks and her mouth pops open. "Fuck it. Bye, Quinn. Thanks for the ride."

The door slams with a loud *bang*. I watch her walk up the driveway, her steps hurried but more steady than before. I'm a little less worried about her condition, now that she seems to be sobering up. She'll be fine. She might not even remember any of this.

For her sake, that would be for the best.

But for my sake? I'm pretty damn agitated about the condition she's left *me* in.

Far worse off than before she put that imagery in my already fucked-up head.

CHAPTER 3

INSIDES

AVERY

Marcy Beloff, victim number one, lies lifeless and cold on the slab.

I never used to number the vics. I was more personable than that. At least, I thought I was. A sensitive medical examiner who cared. Who wanted to make a difference. Who wanted to discover cutting-edge ways to solve crimes and give victims the final say.

But that was before I became a victim myself.

Now, each and every victim that is wheeled into my lab gets identified with a number. The count began after I was abducted and rescued. As if I was starting over. My career. My life. Everything.

The count began when I examined Price Alexander Wells: victim zero.

The Watcher.

The monster who tortured me.

Of course, on paper, he wasn't labeled a vic. On paper he died of a toxic overdose of saxitoxin due to ingesting shellfish. My official examination stated: accident.

The world will never know the evil that monster inflicted. The truth of it is buried with him, all his secrets…and mine. My corrupt part in the disposal of my abductor gave me—the victim—the final say.

In that way, he was my ground zero. The shattered and decimated ruin from where my new life began.

Once you've stared into the dead eyes of your tormenter, seen his insides filled with falsifying evidence, and stamped your name on the COD report to conceal his murder… Well, there's really no turning back.

This is what starting over looks like. This is what becoming a stranger to yourself feels like. This must've been what Sadie suffered all those years ago, and why I could never truly reach her. Or communicate with her. No matter how hard I tried, there was always a noticeable barrier between us. Just a sliver of glass that I could look through and glimpse the person, but not touch.

I turn and stare into the mirror along the wall. And as I look at myself—pale blond hair, skin faded against a white lab coat—I can actually sense the glass between me and my reflection. A thin pane that I should be able to see right through, but somehow, I now notice all the imperfections distorting my image.

Maybe they were there before, and I just never noticed them until now. Somehow the veil was lifted while I was trapped in the hull of that sailboat. I see more clearly than ever before.

I hate it.

Ignorance of our own fractured existence is bliss.

With a sigh, I reach into my pocket and bring out my scar gel. I dab the gel along the healed over cut, my finger tracing the beveled skin of my lip and the soft tissue above my chin. It's faded from an angry red to pink, and will eventually be white—but the scar will never fully disappear. This imperfection *is* skin deep. A permanent reminder.

I sustained other lacerations and scars, smaller blemishes covering my body, but those I can conceal. And in time, they will no longer be noticeable. My abductor knew what he was doing when he sliced my face. He took his time, drawing out the agony, staring into my eyes as he carved my skin.

I wasn't supposed to survive, but in the event that I did, he made sure I'd forever carry his mark.

I close my eyes, inhale a deep breath laced with the chemical scents of the crime lab, and turn toward the vic on the slab, reminding myself why I came back. Why I'm here—why I'm choosing to relive this every day—instead of working at the state of the art pathology lab in New York City.

The offer came in shortly before I was abducted. Back then, there was no hesitancy in my blunt but gracious refusal. I was doing the work I believed in already. I was making a difference right here near the heart of the country.

On the day I returned home, I stared at that letter for hours until the words blurred. It's all still a blur—but the one clear understanding in that moment was that I could not run away. Regardless if Wells is dead…despite the fact that I no longer fear him…retreating from my own lab would be letting him win in the end.

He will not win.

The soft thud of footsteps echos from the hallway beyond the swing doors, and I pull my clipboard to my chest, as if I can somehow hide behind it. I despise this feeling more than anything; I never used to be so fearful.

The doors swing in and Detective Carson enters, all business and cocky smiles. At least he doesn't tiptoe around me. I can say that for him. Carson's arrogance rubs most of the other detectives the wrong way, but his selfishness is refreshing. He's too invested in his own self-importance to bother treating me like a fragile victim.

"Hey, Avery. You got an update on our vic yet?"

No phony pleasantries. No inquiry on my day, or my health. No regard for my mental state whatsoever. Just right to business.

With a curt nod, I pry the clipboard away from my chest

and give it my full attention. "Marcy Beloff. Twenty-five. Single. Lived in Arlington for a year—"

"Sounds like a personal ad," Carson interrupts.

And then there's that. My eyes flick up and pin him with a glare. He clears his throat and rocks back on his heels, sinking his hands into his slack pockets. "Sorry," he says. "Too soon?"

With a heavy exhale, I relax my shoulders. "No. I'm just a little on edge today. It's fine. Make all the jokes you want at the victim's expense."

My slight doesn't faze him, and he nods as I look back down at the report.

I continue going over the victim's basic information, content that Carson has no interest in prying into my personal affairs. He just assumes—as everyone does—that my *on edge* remark is due to my being here, in the lab where I was abducted. Not to mention having been bound and tortured. Possibly even raped...though no one has outright asked.

And yes, I'm still feeling quite on edge for all those reasons, but today, it's a little worse. Because Quinn was a witness to my appalling behavior last night. I've been waiting for him to make an appearance all morning to inquire about the vic—just waiting to see his downturned mouth, the sad, weighty slope of his shoulders, the judgment in his hazel eyes as they refuse to meet mine.

I don't know why it should bother me what Quinn thinks, but it does. I actually don't care if the whole department—

Carson included—gossips behind my back. Speculating about how it's perfectly normal for someone who just suffered a traumatic event to act out in a completely abnormal way. How do they even know it's abnormal?

Maybe I've always drank myself into a blackout and digested concentrated aphrodisiacs. What if I've always had issues getting sexually aroused and needed to get pass-the-fuck-out drunk in order to let loose and have some fun? They don't know me. Not on that level.

My internal rant stops abruptly as Carson says, "Jesus, Avery. You all right?" He steps around the slab to stand beside me. "You look pale. We can do this later—"

"I'm fine. Just tired." I attempt a smile, but I can feel how awkward it is on my wobbly lips. Out of habit that is of late, I cover my mouth with my hand. "Let's just get through this."

"All right. Your call." He gives me another close inspection, his head tilted in that concerned way, before he aims his gaze on the vic.

The fact that I'm so out of sorts that I triggered Carson's notice isn't good. To anyone else, it's probably more than obvious that I'm way off my game. I should've called in sick, but Avery Johnson—the Avery Johnson before the abduction—does not take sick days. I need to focus on work. I just have to push through it until it all clicks back into place.

It has to.

Blowing out a long breath, I pull it together. "Despite the

numerous contusions and lacerations covering her face and body, COD was exsanguination due to a puncture in her abdomen that resulted in liver damage." I set the clipboard down and slip on a pair of gloves. "PAT—"

"What's that?" Carson interrupts.

"Penetrating abdominal trauma," I say as I peel back the white sheet to display the injury. "Sharp force trauma on the left side of her abdomen. The object was small and thin."

"A knife?"

I shake my head. "Hard to say. Possibly. It's obvious that she was attacked. Bruising to her forearms suggests defensive wounds. The contusion below her right eye was in the stages of healing. She'd sustained a battering a few times over." I swallow past the bile rising to my throat.

"I swabbed the wound and sent it out for analysis," I continue. "And I'm running a tox screen to cover all the bases. Waiting on results now."

Carson nods. "It's possible the person delivering the punches is someone different than the perp who inflicted the killing blow. Any way you can distinguish the difference between her defensive wounds and the antemortem bruising?"

Damn. How did I not think of that? I look up at Carson and frown. "Yes. I'll get a complete workup on that next." Glancing down at the vic, I tilt my head. "She suffered a slow and painful death. Her injury could've easily been treated."

A low hum fills the lab as silence builds. Then: "How long

did she suffer?"

"A week…maybe longer. The darkened skin along her abdomen developed days ago."

"She might've assumed it was bruises from the attack. Maybe she'd gotten used to the sight of them. The pain."

I shake my head. "There's no evidence she was struck in her midsection. No. This is from her abdominal cavity filling with blood. She probably suffered hypovolemic shock and inflammation due to blood pooling. She ran a fever. She groaned in pain. She held her stomach and winced at any sudden move. And she wasn't alone. Someone watched her die."

"Avery."

Carson's somber tone draws my attention. I look up to see the unsaid question in his eyes. "We don't know that she was tortured," he says.

I nod once. "But we do know she was abused."

The air thickens, a heavy weight of apprehension settles between us.

"I'll get the toxicology results to you soon," I say, breaking the uncomfortable silence. "By this afternoon. I'll have more definitive answers for you and Quinn then."

I turn away and begin jotting notes on my form, my back to Carson. He accepts the curt dismissal and heads toward the swing doors, but says on his way out, "It will get easier."

My eyes close. A tremor spasms my hand, and the pen

drags down the middle of the page. I look down and study the jagged ink trail as the flapping of the doors echoes through the room.

Easier. With time, everything becomes easier. Our senses dull. Our memory fades. Our pain becomes not as sharp. Then we're not so aware of the displacement we feel in our own lives; how we no longer fit.

Sure. With time, it got easier for Sadie. So easy, in fact, that she justified taking a life with hardly any confliction. Maybe I should've waited for the dulling of time to wipe me void of conscience before I stamped my name on that COD report. Instead, all my wounds remain fresh and unhealed, my guilt a wave of saltwater rushing over.

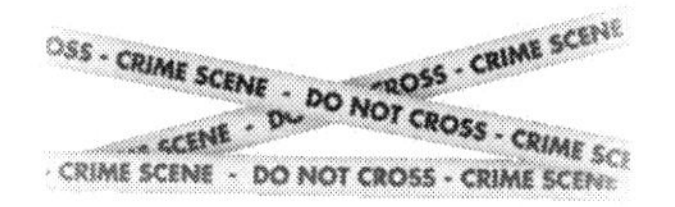

"Do you know how I'll break you?" His words slither into my ear, his breath hot against my face. "It's a slow and laborious process. Not unlike how our Sadie herself was broken. In the end, you'll crave my touch."

The soft pads of his fingers graze me through the sheer material of my underwear. I yank back, my muffled cry gagged by the tape covering my mouth.

His arm slips around my waist, hauling my back against his solid form. Gloved fingers splay against my skin with clinical precision. Everything about him is cold and sterile. "Yes. You'll crave my tender touch…because the alternative is so much worse."

A *bang* rouses me awake with a start. I'm off the cot and through the office door, my heart stuttering in my chest. Quinn and Carson stand in the middle of the lab, Carson hunched over as he picks up a steel brain pan from the floor.

"Sorry," Quinn says, nodding toward the other detective. "The rookie is still acquiring his sleuthing skills." He gives Carson a hard glare before his hazel eyes settle on me.

I look away, finding my phone in my pocket to check the time: 7:35. "I didn't realize how late it was. I just laid down for a minute."

Quinn shrugs. "You've been heading up the lab on your own today."

It's not a question, or an accusation. It's an assessment. I am tired due to the fact that it's a bank holiday and most of my colleagues and interns took half the day off. I didn't want to spend another day in front of the TV. Or sitting alone in the mocking silence. I'd rather be at work, with the dead. At least in their company, I feel a kinship.

We're both numb.

"I still should've gotten you over my findings earlier." I tug out a pair of gloves and switch on the overhead projection screen. An illuminated image of the vic's torso displays. "I'm still examining the trace I found in the wound, but as you can see here"—I point to the puncture mark—"the tear in the liver isn't consistent with a knife. The bruising and perimortem inflammation around her midsection prevented me from determining the exact shape and size of the injury. But the liver still retains the shape."

I bring out the bin containing the damaged organ and place it on the autopsy table.

Quinn moves closer to inspect. "The weapon used was round."

"Like a pen, or pencil," I note.

His gaze sweeps over the projected X-ray, then lands on me. "The perp attacked her with a pen?"

I shrug. "Possibly. Or it could've been an accident."

Carson interjects. "Everything about her circumstance indicates this was no accident."

I agree, for the most part, but… "The injury could've been obtained during a struggle. She may've landed on the object either during or after the assault. There's no way to know for sure."

"Either way," Quinn says, coming around the autopsy cart toward me. "The vic died as a result. We're looking for a perp."

I nod slowly. "I'll see if I can narrow down likely objects. Find the weapon, and I'm sure you'll find your perp."

My gaze holds his a moment too long, and before I can turn away, he says, "Carson, get the techs to dig up the vic's most recent contacts. I want a full report on her job, boyfriends, friends, shopping habits. I'll meet you at the dumpsite in an hour."

From my peripheral, I glimpse the hike of Carson's eyebrows. But he doesn't question his orders. "Right," Carson says. "I'm on it. Meet up in an hour." Then he tucks away his black notepad—the same kind Quinn carries—and exits the lab.

I lick my lips, conscious of the fact I forgot to reapply concealer, as Quinn's penetrating detective gaze borders on invasive. "Something else you need, detective?" I ask, forcing myself to blink in what I hope is a natural way.

His shoulders rise and fall in an easy shrug. "We should talk about last night."

An ache pulses at my temples. "Nothing to talk about. I got a little drunk, but that's not a crime. Is it?"

"No," he says, taking another step closer. "But I am curious about the baggie." He pulls an evidence bag from his pocket. Inside is the remnants of my most recent cocktail.

I yank my gloves off and shove them into my lab coat pockets. "I guess I should thank you for coming to me instead of pressing charges." Then I reconsider the evidence bag. "Unless that's why you're here. To arrest me."

His features contort, his expression incensed. "I'm not one to pry, Avery. But when my lead M.E. is waving drugs around in public—"

"It's not drugs," I correct. "At least, not the kind you're assuming."

He visibly relaxes, if only a fraction. "Then why don't you clarify."

I brace my hands on the edge of the autopsy cart. "Because it's none of your business."

"Are you still seeing a therapist?"

His question throws me. "What?"

"You're required to see an in-house counselor. It's a condition of your remittance." He steps closer. I push away from the cart. "You're not a cop, but you are a part of the team. If any one of my guys went through what you did..." he trails off. "Let's just say, I look out for my own. And I consider you one of mine."

His words sink past my defenses. For a moment, I feel the press of his concern, his burden. I'm hit with the memory of the callused roughness of his hand as it held mine, the contrasting tenderness of his touch. It strips me of my anger, and my body feels weak. Like it's taking all my strength just to stand.

"I stopped seeing her," I say. "The therapist. It wasn't helping."

"And you started self medicating," he concludes.

And like that, my defenses go up. Before Quinn is anything to me—friend, ally, colleague—he's first a cop. I know that it was more than his duty to help rescue me—that the whole precinct felt my abduction on a personal level—but I lost that connection to them down in the hell pit of that boat.

I lost the part of myself that fought the good fight. What

Quinn and I had in common. I no longer see the world as he does; in black and white. Good guys and bad. Right and absolute wrong. I'm lost somewhere in the murky shades. For that alone, he can't reach me. No matter how far he extends the branch.

There's only one person I know that understands me on this new plane of suffering. And when I look at her now, I glimpse the monstrous, distorted reflection of myself. It's painful—but it's brutal honesty.

I don't blame Sadie. Rather, in some completely fucked up way, I loathe her for revealing this side of myself. I think she realizes that. Because the moment I stepped foot in the precinct, she took her overdue vacation time. Every day of it. Something so out of character for her.

Maybe she's giving me time to…adjust. Or she's afraid that I'm not strong enough to carry the weight of this secret—that I'll break. But the truth is, I was already broken. Framing a shellfish for Wells' death was just a result of the damage. I can't blame Sadie for my actions.

I would do it again.

And faced with the choice, I believe I would be the one to end his life.

"I've seen that look before," Quinn says.

Shaken out of my reverie, I lift my gaze to his. Find his hazel eyes studying me. I'm very aware of the *look* I'm projecting this second, but I say, "What look?"

Quinn leans against the wall and laces his arms over his broad chest. "That stubborn one. Bonds had that same look in the hospital when we were waiting to hear on your condition. It's one that says no matter how hard I present my case, your mind is already made up."

I ease out a shaky breath past trembling lips. "How is Sadie?" I turn around, making myself busy with replacing the vic's liver in the wall locker. Hoping he takes the bait and changes the subject.

"Still on leave," he says. His voice grows closer, causing my hands to slick with sweat. I take out my gloves and force them on. "But you know that. You two are close. I'm sure she's already told you the same thing I am now."

In an instant, Quinn has me turned to face him, his strong hands anchored to my arms. "That whatever you're going through—something I know I have no right to even imagine—you need help, Avery. You can't hide from it, and no amount of alcohol or drugs can make it vanish."

I try to pull out of his grip, but his hold is solid. I'm desperate to be away from his shrewd gaze. "You don't know your partner as well as you think, Quinn. And you know nothing about me or what I'm going through." Finally, I tear out of his hold as the shock of my words seizes him.

"You said something to that effect last night."

Backing away, I put even more distance between us. "Then you should probably hear me clearly by now. I don't need a hero to swoop in and save me. And I'm pretty sure Sadie doesn't, either. Besides, she's found someone, Quinn. You need to let it go."

My accusation hits him like a slap across the face, and for a second, regret tears through me. "Right," he recovers quickly. "You must think I'm pretty transparent."

I shrug, my body and mind exhausted. "Next time you come here, keep focused on the job."

"You called *me* last night, remember?" His eyebrows hike.

"You're right—I'm sorry. I made a mistake."

My harsh declaration hangs heavily in the lab as I turn my back to Quinn. I can still feel his penetrating stare as I push through the double doors. I force my feet to keep going. If I don't get enough distance between us, I'll turn back, and I'm not strong enough to keep up this front with Quinn much longer.

CHAPTER 4

THE JOB

QUINN

Keep focused on the job. Damn straight I am.

I'm tired of being on edge around the trim in my department. *Fucking women.*

Avery's given me permission to let it go—and so that's what I'm doing. She's a big girl. She knows better than anyone what she needs. And she's made it clear that I can't help. No surprise there. I'm just relieved I'm off the hook.

Now I can get back to doing what I do best.

I steer toward the crime scene where yellow tape marks off the Dumpster on the alley side of 11th Street. The fact that the perp chose a fucking Dumpster as the body dumpsite ratchets up my annoyance. It's unimaginative.

As I park, I observe the area. It's a high-end type atmosphere. The Dumpster is shared by a couple of restaurants and one bar. The bar, or *lounge*, is a swanky lawyer joint set amid the Courthouse Metro District.

I can read a lot into the perp just by his selection process—or *lack* of process—of the dumpsite, but I can't deny that I'm missing Sadie's extra observant insight into the perp's behavior right about now.

I scroll through my contacts until I come up on her name. She left specific instructions to contact her with anything imperative. My thumb hovers over her name, ready to put that into effect, but Avery's accusation bleeds into my conscience. Dammit.

Instead, I click off the screen and climb out of my Crown Vic, shaking off my moment of weakness.

That's all it is. Weakness. There's nothing about this case that the department can't handle. That *I* can't handle. Until I decide my next move, I need to get used to working without a partner.

I spot Carson talking to a waitress near the dumpsite. Yeah, he's working the case all right. Working that waitress with the short skirt real well.

I clear my throat as I sidle up beside him.

His back visibly straightens. "Thank you for your time, Melody."

The girl tosses her head, clearing the bright pink and red streaks of hair from her eyes, then stubs out her cigarette with the toe of her boot. "Yeah, no problem. Like I said, I'm not sticking around here much longer. Hope you catch the creep."

I hold up a hand, halting her retreat. "Miss, one more second. Please."

"Make it half a second, duce. I gotta get my girl to her gig." She nods to another young woman sporting an even shorter jean skirt seated on a motorcycle.

We interviewed everyone from the adjourning businesses last night, canvassed the nearby neighborhood today, but somehow missed this one waitress. "Were you working last night?"

She shakes her head. "No. Like I told your partner here, I've only been in Arlington for a couple of days. Tonight's my first shift, thanks to a friend who got me the hookup." She glances around the alley. "But to be honest, I don't need this crazy-ass, serial killer shit you guys got going on here. Not in my life. Soon as I heard the news…" She throws up her hands. "We're riding out tonight after Dar's shift."

Smart girl. "Safe travels."

"Thanks, duce," she says with a wink, then heads off toward her bike.

There's a look of longing on Carson's face as he watches the biker girl leave. I have to admit, I don't blame him. It is tempting… Maybe twenty years ago tempting for me.

He's making the right call, though. He could've held her here for another twenty-four hours. Longer if he pressed the full charges. The white powder coating the tip of her nose and the jacked-up tremble of her hands are dead giveaways.

"Glad to see you got the right head in the game," I say, drawing his attention away from the girl.

He jerks his head back, feigning ignorance. "I don't have time to waste on simple possession charges. Not with another murder hitting headlines."

I let it ride. He knows I'm talking about more than popping the girl with a drug charge, but neither of us are going there.

"You learn anything new?" I ask, heading back around to the other side of the Dumpster. CSU already processed the scene last night, but that was before the ME had any info on the possible murder weapon. I read through the reports, looking for any mention of pens, pencils…any circular object that could've been tossed in the Dumpster with the vic. Nothing of the like made it into the CSU reports.

Doesn't mean that there's not something here, however. I don't envy the CSU crew, Dumpster diving into the early hours of the morning, picking through garbage and rotten food. My nostrils flare as I lean over the edge and get a rank whiff.

"Besides the fact that I'm too old for biker chicks?" Carson says, and I send an impatient glare his way. "Yeah, I did. Melody said she recognized the vic from her picture on the wall inside the bar." He points toward The Cosmo. "I figured I'd go check it out. Find out why the rest of the staff failed to mention she was a regular."

This piques my interest. "I'll go with you."

Inside the bar, I let Carson question the bartender while

I get an impression of the place. Dim, multicolored track lighting highlights crimson leather-backed chairs and white marble counters. Cherry oak tables match the hardwood flooring. It says "money."

It's the kind of bar that let's you know you're spending a hefty wad just walking into the place. In the corner near the floor-to-ceiling window, a group of suits stand around a tall table, doing just that.

I stroll toward them, picking up on their conversation before they make me. Their discussion of the recent murder dies abruptly.

"Gentlemen," I say, reaching inside the inseam of my trench coat to produce my badge. "I need a moment of your time."

The leader of the pack makes himself known immediately. "This in regard to Marcy Beloff?"

I hold my poker face. "You know the victim?"

"No. Not at all. Just an educated guess," he says, motioning the hand holding a tumbler toward the yellow tape marking off a section of the side door.

"Right." I glance over at the door, then look at him. "But normally strangers don't refer to a victim by name. I believe you're educated enough to understand my leap there. What are you…?" I take in their faces; clean shaven, soft as a baby's butt. "Post grad? First year interns just passed the bar?"

I hate lawyers. I especially can't stand cocky little yuppie lawyers living off their trust funds. They waste my time, get in the way, and make my job harder. All of them—every single slimy one—bend the law. And not for their client's sake; so they can get their headline claim to fame for when they run for the Commonwealth.

"I'm second year," trust fund says. His eyes narrow. "And I happen to always refer to the 'vic' by name. I find it helps me remember they're a person who deserves justice, instead of just another victim whose case I need to close out to meet my monthly quota."

I raise my eyebrows. So trust fund has some experience—and some balls. I let the jibe go and bring out my notepad. "Were you and your party here last night?"

"We're here nearly every evening," one of the even younger looking lawyers says. "The firm is a couple blocks away."

Noted. I look up. "Then I gather you've seen Marcy Beloff in here before."

Vacant stares.

"Come on, guys," I say, pointing toward the wall of framed photographs behind the counter. "You're here every night, and not a one of you have laid eyes on a woman who's obviously in here enough to make the wall of fame?"

Trust fund clears his throat. "Listen. I don't know anything about her. Never seen her—but that's because I doubt the pic was taken for her sake." At my pinched brow, he adds, "Ryland Maddox. The guy in the photo with her. I'm sure that's how she got up there."

A familiar itch tickles the back of my head.

"Hotshot attorney who just made partner at Lark and Gannet," he continues. "Maddox has a different girl on his arm at any given time, so I wouldn't read too much into it."

Maddox. The face in the photo clicks with the name, and tension grips my shoulders. Captain Wexler had a run-in with this guy a couple months back. Maddox got a felony offender off on a technicality. The charge: rape.

An ugly picture is starting to develop, and I don't like how this puzzle is piecing itself together. I make a note to pull all the cases Maddox was appointed to before I jot down all the lawyers' names and relieve them of my company.

I meet Carson at the door. "Looks like our vic was a high dollar call girl," he says as we exit the bar. "At least, that's what I gathered from the bartender. Once he recognized her in the pic with some rich lawyer, he claimed she catered to big names in the city."

A prostitute murdered—or possibly an accidental death, according to Avery—and dumped in the alley where her possible rich clients frequent.

There's too many possibilities, too many weak theories in that scenario, and not enough substantial evidence to make a case. Without a murder weapon, we're just pissing in the wind. And that stank breeze is blowing around a lot of key players.

Which never ends well.

"We need to have our shit in order before we take this to Wexler," I say. I click the key fob and open my car door, turn toward Carson. "I want files on Maddox. Keep any investigation into him low-key. If the press gets word of this—"

"I got it." Carson holds up a hand. "These upper crust douchebags will make the department look like idiots."

"That would be the least painful consequence," I mutter as I climb into my Crown Vic.

I sit for a minute and watch Carson track back through the alley toward his car. When I see his taillights fade, I pull onto the main road, confident I'm making yet another mistake.

But with where my career is heading, what difference does one more make?

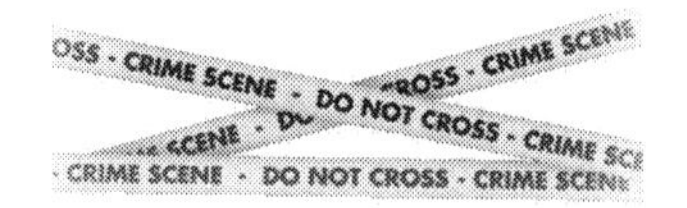

Avery's porch light is on. The lights inside are off, but the glow of the TV pulses against the drawn shades. I should wait until tomorrow. There's no new evidence, not really, and she was exhausted earlier.

I should back out of her driveway.

But I don't. The state she was in last night has me concerned. And so here I am, watching her house. Making sure she's safe. At least, that's what I tell myself as I sit here sipping a fresh cup of coffee at nearly ten o'clock at night. Staring at her windows, checking for signs of life. Like a fucking stalker.

I groan and shift in my seat, setting the cup inside the holder. This was easier when I had a legitimate excuse, like visiting her in the hospital. What the hell am I doing here now?

I grip the door handle, deciding that I do have new evidence to present. Avery can confirm if the vic was a pro. There are telltale signs that every prostitute exhibits; drawbacks of the *job*. Prostitution has its own occupational hazards.

And if our vic was a pro, that's going to open up a huge investigation into her johns. I should get started on that right away. Get ahead of the press.

I've made my decision and am slowly making my way up the front porch when the door opens. I stop on the third step, shove my hands into my pockets.

"Quinn? What the hell?"

Avery stands in the doorway, a black silky-thing of a robe draped around her body. Her blond hair is pulled up in one of those messy buns, loose wisps falling around her eyes and shoulders. I get a glimpse of her legs through the cracked doorway, and have to force my gaze up to meet her eyes—which are glaring at me something fierce.

I clear my throat. "Had a break in the case," I say, which is a clear exaggeration for what Carson and I uncovered. "Thought we could go over a couple of things before tomorrow. Get a jump on—"

"You're so full of it." She shakes her head. "A break in the case, huh."

"Yes."

Her deep brown eyes don't waver. "And just how is this case any different than the others?" At my obvious loss to her question, she clarifies. "You've never shown up at my house in the middle of the night before. Actually, you've never shown up at my house *ever*. Even when we were working the serial murders," she says, glancing down before lifting her gaze to mine again. "Go home, Quinn."

Her harsh assessment stings, but it's dead on. This isn't about the case. I'm not entirely sure what it's about...but the case hasn't brought me to her door tonight.

"Sorry to have bothered you." I step down, ready to end my humiliation, when the signs stop my retreat. Fresh makeup. Not worn or removed, like someone getting ready for bed. Dangly, silver earrings showing through her loose tresses, and a bra strap peeking from beneath the robe.

I might be clueless when it comes to women in general, but I'm not completely blind. I knew when Jenna was lying, and I don't need my keen detective instincts to see that Avery is hiding something now.

My mouth pops open to inquire, but a loud noise coming from inside snaps it shut. I'm already marching up the porch and pressing against the wood paneling of the door. "Let me in, Avery."

Her eyes widen. Whether in fear or hesitancy, I'm not sure. But she's desperate to keep me from entering. I tower over her and pull my stubborn gaze away from her to stare into the darkened living room where two guys are hustling to get their shit together.

I hear one of them say, "Cop…" and that's when I delicately maneuver Avery aside and push the door open. "Stop right—" I reach for my badge, but Avery clasps my forearm with a tight grip.

"Quinn, you can't shoot them—"

And like that, the guys are hauling ass toward the back door and I'm staring down at her stunned face. "I'm not pulling my gun. Jesus, Avery."

She releases a clipped breath and drops her hands. She's shaking.

"What's going on here?" I let my gaze travel around the dark room. Flatscreen on but muted; a topless girl giving a lap dance on the screen. A couple candles lit on an end table. On the other table, there's another one of those baggies.

Avery follows my line of sight. "It's not what you think…"

"You keep saying that." I walk toward the table and take out a pen from my inseam to pick it up by the corner. "But if you really want me to believe you, then you need to talk." My instincts say that I don't actually want to know—that I've interrupted some kind of kinky sex party…and I really don't need that image of Avery in my mind.

I hear her force out a long breath before she picks up the remote and clicks off the TV. She walks over to the end table, blows out the candles, and flips on the lamp. The room fills with a light. "It's an aphrodisiac."

This isn't what I expect. Cocaine, molly, meth—all drugs I know about and how to handle when it comes to the user. What the fuck is an aphrodisiac? "Like Spanish fly?"

I face Avery and glimpse a hint of her smile. "Wow. You are old school. Spanish fly," she repeats with mock humor as she sinks onto the couch. "No. Yes…it's something in the realm, but more potent. Think red wine and chocolate on crack," she says, pulling her robe more securely around her chest.

I lay the baggie on the table and pocket my pen. My mind starts deducing the facts. I can't help it; there's no Off switch for the detective in me. Avery has a boyfriend. At least, that's been the gossip around the department. She keeps to herself, always professional, but I run a mental tab on everyone.

I'm sure transitioning back into her life hasn't been easy since the abduction, but what I've seen of her the past couple of days goes against the grain of the Avery Johnson I know.

"And the two guys…?" I prompt.

She shrugs. "I tried to make it work with Rick," she says, confirming my suspicion about the boyfriend. "He was so accepting. Completely willing to wait. Never pressuring me for—" she breaks off and looks up at me. "Sex."

This conversation is entering a territory beyond my comfort zone. I shift my feet, glance back at the door, wondering if it's too late to flee. Only as I look at Avery, I know

I'm not going anywhere.

The downturned corners of her full lips is like a force reeling me in, and my feet are moving me toward her. "What a bastard," I say, pleased when another small smile graces her mouth.

But she quickly covers it with her hand. "It wasn't him," she continues. "It was me. I just wanted everything to be normal again. I wanted to pick up where we left off. But being with him, seeing the commiseration in his eyes, the delicate way he handled me…it was a constant reminder that I'm broken. That I must now be treated differently."

I try to think of something to say, wanting to denounce her very inaccurate assessment of herself, but she pushes past her statement. "Anyway," she says, sitting forward and propping her elbows on her knees. "The two guys here…the guys at the bar last night…I don't know them. They don't know me. They have no knowledge of what I went through. I don't see my pain reflected back at me in their eyes. Just lust. They just want me. And it…helps." She lowers her gaze.

I tread carefully. "If that's so, then why the need for an aphrodisiac?"

She visibly squirms. "I said that I wanted to *be* normal, not that I magically *am*. Ending things with Rick helped to forget some, but I still…" Her eyes capture mine. "Do you really want to hear all this, Quinn?"

She's giving me an out. We work together, know certain

details of each other's lives, but there's a line colleagues don't cross. *Shouldn't* cross. Once I go to that next level, once I offer myself as a confidant, it's as good as making a promise to her. Which comes with a clause that gives her access to the intimate details of *my* life. These exchanges are never one-sided.

I glance around the room, seeking evidence that she already has a confidant. Pictures of parents, friends—but it's disturbing how bare her walls are. They look like mine. Blank white slates. One obvious drawback of our careers is that they don't leave much room for nurturing relationships.

I'm moving before I've even fully made a decision. Because, if I'm being honest with myself, I already crossed that line the first night I slipped into her hospital room despite the nurse's bitching about visiting hours and took her hand. When I brushed my fingers through her hair to calm her as she fought sleep, screaming against her nightmares.

I lower myself before her, eye-to-eye. "Yes."

The glassy whites of her eyes shimmer in the dim lighting. Pressing her lips together, she sniffs hard, fortifying herself. "Okay." She nods. "It's like, I'm disgusted with myself because I can't stop thinking about sex. Wanting to prove that what he did to me…that it didn't ruin me. I need to have control over my body—to be able to get turned on and *want* to have sex when I say so. I want a man to touch me and not cringe at that touch. I want to stop flinching at something as harmless as a kiss. I want to close my eyes and not see his twisted smile. Not feel him…"

Her whole body is trembling. I move onto the couch and just sit next to her. It's Avery who presses into my chest, clings to the lapels of my coat. My arms surround her of their own accord, and I let my chin rest on top of her head.

Having engrossed myself with the sadistic details of each of the serial killings in order to get inside the head of the man I was hunting, I know all the sick and twisted ways he tormented his victims. And when Avery was laying in that hospital bed, my mind spun on a continuous loop, like an old 70s movie reel. Envisioning her torment.

When it came time to interview her, it wasn't me. If I confirmed the images in my head, I would never stop seeing them. Every time I'd look at her in the lab, I'd see her as a victim. And the perp was dead. I couldn't kill him twice.

I can't make her pain stop now. I can't fix this for her. What the fuck good am I?

Her petite body has stopped shivering, her limbs going lax against my chest. "He didn't even rape me," she whispers.

I bite down on my lip. Dammit. She sounds just like a vic. "But he did, Avery. He raped your life. He tore your security and faith away."

She shakes her head against me. "How can I be this fucked up when he didn't even get that far? The whole time, no matter what he did, I kept telling myself that it wasn't that bad, as long as he didn't actually rape or kill me. That I was surviving."

I pull her tighter to me. "You stayed strong. Avery, I can't think of another woman who could've… You're the strongest woman I know. God, before we got to you, I was terrified of finding the worst." I brush her hair aside, my thumb wiping away the gathered tears under her eye. "Then I was amazed. You were still Avery. Even in the pit of hell, you lashed out against it. You defied it. And you were still that same, vibrant woman. You still are now."

Her breath whispers past her lips, a soft exhale that draws me in. "I don't feel so strong."

My gaze travels over her face, and as she presses nearer, her eyes close. I can feel her breath against my mouth. *Taste her, just once…* A chorus thrums inside my head. I would covet that taste. I would worship this woman with one kiss and dispel every abhorrent lie festering inside her beautiful head—but it's wrong.

I pull away just as she tilts her head back. I clear my throat, breaking the connection. Her eyes snap open.

"Sadistic shits like Simon feed off of weakness." I draw back to look at her. "He couldn't break you. You're not broken. You're here now because of that strength that he couldn't tear down."

She blinks. "Simon," she says slowly, sounding out the word, as if it's the first time she's uttered her former lab tech's name.

My brow furrows. "He wasn't just a perp, Avery. He was

someone you knew. Someone you trusted. It's understandable that this process is even more difficult because of that fact."

Releasing a strained breath, she nods. "You're right. Of course." She nods again, pushing herself even farther out of my grasp. "You should go. I should get some sleep."

And suddenly, she's too far away.

I run my palms over my slacks, then stand. "Right."

Pieces start connecting, but I'm not sure I want them to. Avery is a colleague. I need to get that through my fucking head. I'm desperate to resurrect that very high wall I always keep in place. "But first. Is it safe?" I say, needing to know this much. "This aphrodisiac. Where are you getting it from?"

"God, Quinn. Yes, it's safe. I engineered it." She reaches over and grabs the baggie. "Most of the compounds are organic. It's simple enough, really. But I did have to…"

I tilt my head. "Have to what?"

Her slim throat bobs on a swallow. "I needed something that I couldn't get myself. It's not bad. It's just blacklisted by the FDA. It's dumb, really. Damn activists." She shakes her head.

"What?"

She hesitates, then: "I had to go through the darknet to obtain ambergris, which I in turn extracted and produced ambrein—the main ingredient in my cocktail."

She might as well be speaking Greek. I know Avery's smart, capable of more than simply determining cause of death for victims, but this just proves how the department takes her intelligence for granted.

"Sum it up for the old-school detective, Aves. Please."

"Sperm whale vomit, Quinn." She raises her eyebrows. "Okay? It sounds horrid, but it's been used for centuries as incense and in perfumes. And it's quite coveted now, damn near impossible to get, even though the contact I go through obtains it naturally. Collecting aged ambergris off the shore of Africa rather than extracting it violently. The way barbaric whale hunters do."

"So you're digesting whale vomit?" How the hell did we take this turn? "And you're going through illegal channels to get it. This is dangerous—"

"You're so...black and white. God, it never used to bother me before. I respect your methods, Quinn. But on this? You couldn't be more wrong." She stands then, decidedly ending our conversation.

Before I leave, I have to put away one last thing. "What's the exchange?"

Her shoulders tense. With her back to me, she says, "Not money. My income doesn't allow for such extravagance. So I have an arrangement."

My cop hackles raise. "And the arrangement is...?"

She turns toward me. "I give them a cut of the mix."

"You're giving these people a powerful aphrodisiac to dispense at their will without even finding out what they're doing with it?"

"It's harmless," she insists. "They get a less potent cocktail. It's about as effective as porn. It doesn't strip anybody of their will, Quinn. God, how could you even assume…after what I've been through?"

She takes off toward the kitchen. I'm by her side, grabbing her hand and pulling her to a stop before she's gone. "I didn't assume. But it's my job, Avery."

Her chest rises and falls with her shaky breaths, her robe coming open up top. I should release her and look away, but she's just too beautiful. Her skin flushed, her hair falling loose.

As her gaze drops to our linked hands, she runs her thumb over my knuckles, and a spark of memory tears through me. The feel of her soft skin against mine. I want more of it. I want it *all*.

When her eyes finally meet mine, I glimpse a hint of remembrance there—just a vague flicker that makes me question if she knew I was with her those nights. "I know. Your job," she says, her tone sullen. "The real reason you're here tonight."

The verbal blow knocks me back, and I do let her go. "We used to be on that same page."

She shrugs. "That was before I started playing for the other team." At my wary expression, she says, "Team victim."

Words fail me as she exits the living room. I stare at the floor, hating that I can't make this better for her—that I can't fix it. In the hospital, I felt like her hero, but here in the waking world, her nightmares are real and too complicated for simple reassurances.

"That night," I call out. "I should've carried you."

Within seconds, Avery rounds the corner, her face pinched in question. "What?"

"That night we found you," I repeat, looking into her eyes. "I should've carried you out—"

"Honestly, Quinn, I don't need a hero," she cuts in. "I didn't need one then, and I don't need one now. What I *need* is someone who isn't afraid to touch me in the light of day."

And hell, there it is. She calls me out. The venom in her words should shut me down, but despite my fear of losing control over this situation, I press against her defenses. "I don't want to be your fucking hero, Avery. You don't need saving. But I do regret not being able to protect you—to show you right then in that moment that I'd take on the world to keep you safe."

For a second, her features soften. Her gaze locks with mine, and I can almost reach her. "And why didn't you?" she asks, snapping her damn wall back into place. "Why didn't you swoop in and scoop me into your big detective arms? Because I'm tainted? Because I'm too fragile? Because you're scared to be so close to the sickness?"

"No…never. Because I was terrified. That if I ever wrapped my arms around you, I would never let you go again." I invade her personal space, killing the separation she's put between us.

"And that fucking terrified me."

I watch her swallow, the slender column of her neck so tempting, so delicate. "And now?"

My hands flex at my sides, but I don't reach out, even though every part of me screams to touch her. "I'm still terrified. But I'm here, aren't I? I'll be whatever you need me to be. A friend. A confidant—"

She holds up a hand. Then, touching that hand to the scar along her lip, she shrinks away. "I think what I need is sleep." She turns her back to me, and this time, I let her leave the room for good.

Allowing Avery to have the last word, I take my leave. I've already made a fucking mess of it all, dammit. Before the door closes behind me, she shouts, "What new evidence do you have, Quinn? Remember?"

I stand paused in the doorway. "I need you to determine if the vic was a pro."

Silence stretches out. The distance building between us lodges an ache beneath my chest. Then she appears in the living room. "It's possible," she says. "The vic had a long-term birth control measure in place. And the scarring along her vaginal walls could be due to numerous sexual encounters. Yes. I'd say the possibility is very likely if you have additional evidence to support it."

I nod slowly. "All right. Thanks."

"Is that all you wanted?"

Her question grips me like a vise, crushing my lungs. The truthful response doesn't have a place here, however. I push it down deep, giving her a simple, "Yes," before I shut the door on my way out.

Being in control of my surroundings and myself is what keeps my instincts sharp. I depend on it at all times. But with Avery, I feel that control slipping, weakening more and more every second.

CHAPTER 5

DISCOVERY

AVERY

When I think of how I got to this place in my life, there's no one, defining factor. It must be that way for most people when they recount the many decisions that lead them to a particular point in time when they examine the mess their life has become.

A series of decisions were made, each one branching out a new limb, connecting to a different course. I used to see the whole of my life as a labyrinth. A beautiful but neat and concise warren of graceful curves and paths. I was always so purposeful. Every choice made, I made it with absolution.

But in one dark twist, storm clouds covered my masterpiece and thorn vines clawed at the walls until they crumbled. Leaving behind a dilapidated and warped maze. I can now feel myself panting for breath, bare feet slapping the wrecked path, thorns snagging my ankles, as I search for the exit.

There is no way out.

I've been plunged into a never-ending rotation. Round and round. A nightmare from which I'll never awaken.

Survive.

Like I voiced to Quinn last night, I only had to survive Wells. Just until I was safe again. Then I could reclaim my life. I'd find myself once more.

Only it will never be over. And this fight-or-flight panic coursing through my veins will eventually eat me alive.

"Doctor Johnson, I think I need you to look at this."

Jillian's voice pulls me out of my morbid thoughts. I shake off my conversation with Quinn, reminding myself that he has the best intentions—especially since he doesn't know the truth of my abductor—and address my newest intern. "What do you have?"

She squints into the microscope. "I'm not sure. I don't think I've ever identified anything like this before. Can you look?"

I pull off my blood-covered gloves and toss them into the waste. Hunching over the eyepiece, I close one eye. And that panic races anew, my heart galloping. I stand straight and turn to face her. "Mark it as unknown for now."

Her eyebrows draw together, but she nods. "Yes, ma'am. Should I advise Detective Quinn on the discovery?"

My heartbeat pulses in my ears. "No…not yet. Not until

we can determine the origin."

She seems distressed, as it's protocol to always report any findings—whether we can determine them or not—to the case detectives. As forensic pathologists, that's the job. That's the purpose.

"I'll prepare a sample to send out," she says, getting right on it.

She's a good intern. Bright, diligent, ambitious. She won't let this finding go. It will be a shame if I have to replace her.

"Jillian, place the sample in my locker. I have other trace to send out, as well." I force a smile. "I'll take care of it."

With a bright smile of her own, she flutters off to fulfill her assignment.

Back in my office, I press my hands to the closed door, shutting out the noise of the lab. *I need Sadie.*

Retrieving my phone from my pocket, I scroll to her contact info and tap the screen. The ring seems to drone on forever as my conscience tightens into a suffocating noose.

"This better be about cocktails," Sadie answers.

I swallow down the burn coating my throat. "It is." The very cocktail I developed in my personal lab. At least, a form of it. Someone—a very smart someone—tampered with the structure. But I need time to study the compound to determine how, and to what effect.

"This doesn't sound like fun cocktails," Sadie says. "Avery, is everything okay?"

“I can’t talk. I’m at work right now. Can we meet later?”

“Of course. I have the perfect place.”

Once I hang up, the panic subsides, but only just. After last night, how the hell am I going to explain this to Quinn? How am I going to explain when I don’t even understand how my compound showed up as trace in the vic’s system?

I should take this information to Quinn right now. Get it out in the open and let him investigate. Quinn’s good at his job, and if handing over my darknet contacts means he traces them back to the killer…

Oh, God. If I’m implicated in this investigation, that could call into question all the past cases I’ve personally handled. Which in turn will open up a further investigation into my COD reports—like the report on Wells.

That can’t happen. If it were only my career on the line, I wouldn’t hesitate. But Sadie is connected to that course of action. What she did for me… No. I can’t let her reputation be marred, or *worse*, due to my mistake.

A stupid, stupid mistake.

I snatch my purse off my desk and lock the office door. As I pass Jillian, I give her a quick smile, then snag the tray of samples. “I’ll run these over to forensics on my way out.”

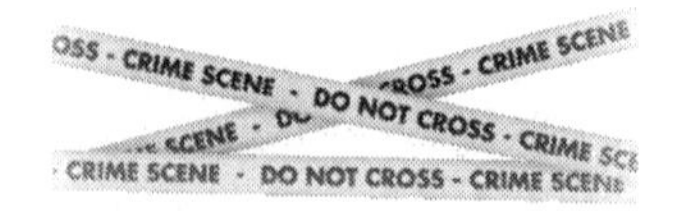

“I only have till tomorrow until the crime lab figures out

these samples never made it to forensics." I hitch the cooler strap higher on my shoulder, securing their safety on my person.

I follow Sadie's lead toward a private area of the club. The Lair isn't my first choice for a confessional, but it's ironically fitting. When admitting to developing a potent aphrodisiac to help stimulate your own dwindling libido, and in turn having inadvertently supplied that drug to possible criminals...where better to confess your sins than a sex club?

Luckily, as it's the middle of the day, the club is closed. Far less chance for anyone to spot me here. There're a couple of people wandering the ground level, unboxing merchandise and setting up displays, but otherwise this is as secluded as it comes. I can't imagine Quinn suddenly popping up in a place like this.

A stage is set before us, with contraptions I couldn't name if I tried. The walls are painted black. It's chilly and quiet and, even though we're alone, I feel as if I'm standing on a platform, about to bare my soul.

"Colton's in his office," she says, pulling out a couple of stools for us around a table. "We're alone."

Her confirmation is encouraging. I trust Sadie. If not for her, Price Alexander Wells—the vile monster—might still be out there. Even with all the evidence we had against him, he still might've gotten off on a lesser charge. I've seen it happen time and time again in the system. Wells was a topnotch lawyer, with other topnotch lawyer and judge contacts. Wells being set free to mutilate, rape, and kill other women wasn't a chance either of us was willing to take.

"I think I screwed up," I say, laying it all out there at once. I tell her about the cocktail, about my darknet contacts. About the ambrein compound that carries my signature. Which has just been discovered in my lab and entered into the chain of evidence for our latest vic.

"It's circumstantial," Sadie declares, her voice level. Through my whole story, she didn't crack once. "What you developed isn't illegal."

"It's not approved by the FDA," I counter.

"Neither are half the cold meds out there, but we consume them just the same." She offers a slight smile. Her green eyes widen with sincerity as she pushes on. "Quinn's a good cop."

I roll my eyes. "Believe me, I know. And damn stubborn when he gets a whiff of something hinky."

She smirks. "He'll get to the bottom of it, Avery. He's like a dog with a bone. You had nothing to do with harming this woman. This is not your fault. And you don't even know how the ambrein compound was entered into her system, or if it has anything at all to do with how she died. Let Quinn do his job and find out. I promise you, he won't let your name be tarnished. Regardless of what you may think, he does want justice, but he wants that justice to come without implicating those he cares for. He will back you up until he finds reason not to…but he will never stop searching for a way to help you. He's a good cop who still believes in other good cops and good people."

I inhale a full breath, then free it, releasing some of the anxiety I've been carrying since I first recognized the compound. "As his partner, I guess you know better than anyone." I raise an eyebrow.

For the first time, I see a flicker of doubt cross her pretty face. "Partner might be a stretch these days. I think the serial case has finally gotten to him. Now that he's had time to process everything."

"You don't think—"

"No," she cuts in. "Even if he did suspect, I'm the one who fabricated the evidence. Not you. It's all on me, Avery. And when the time comes, I'll be the one to confront Quinn on it."

I swallow down my unease. The plan was set. Sadie was to take care of Wells—I didn't ask questions; she made it clear I wasn't going to know the details—and I was responsible for planting the shellfish toxin in his gastrointestinal tract. When the moment came, however, with the monster cold and lifeless on my slab…I froze.

Sadie took over to complete the deed where I failed.

"I owe you so much…*too* much," I tell her. "Had I just been able to—"

"Some dark things in this world we can't unsee," she says, her hand finding mine. "Once it takes root, we only have two choices. Let it consume us, changing us, manipulating us into its likeness, or destroy it." Her grasp tightens. "I'm glad I was there to take the darkness in your place. That you didn't have to make that choice."

I feel the burn of tears behind my eyes, and I hate them. I hate feeling so powerless and weak. "You shouldn't have had to make that choice, either," I say. "Because honestly, Sadie, I fear it's too late. That the things I've seen…what I've suffered…the darkness has already consumed me."

She shakes her head, and a warm smile slants her mouth. "You being here right now, conflicted over what to do, is proof that it hasn't, Avery."

I nod, trying to accept her words, wanting to believe in them. I'm just scared that when I walk out of this club, the choice to do the right thing won't come as easily to me as she believes.

As she walks me toward the exit of the voyeur room, Sadie says, "This is where I met Colton."

I send her an unguarded smile. Sadie is the only person I've never caught staring at my scar. My gaze drops to hers out of reflex; the jagged scar marring her collarbone—the one she has always hidden until now. Whatever has changed for Sadie, whatever reason she has for no longer wishing to conceal it—at least the demon who branded her granted her that option.

"You're lucky you found someone," I say, thinking of how much happier she seems lately.

She pauses at the red rope, turning to face me. "It's also where I first met Wells."

A shiver slithers through my body.

"Good and evil. Yin and Yang," she says. "One doesn't exist without the other. We have to fight our way through that darkness in order to save the things we love the most."

And as I follow her out of the room, I watch Colton greet Sadie in the hallway, immediately taking her into his arms. She belongs there.

I nod to him as I pass, noticing not for the first time how his features only seem to shift to a lighter countenance when she's around. Otherwise, he's every bit as intimidating as his size and striking dark features allude.

"You should come one night," Sadie says before I leave the hallway.

I look around, trying to keep my smile in place. "I think this is a bit out of my depth."

She shrugs. "The invitation is always open."

"All right," I say, and mean it. "Maybe one day soon."

I leave them to adore each other in privacy, deciding I should've sought Sadie's advice on my personal issues before I tried to invent a remedy of my own disastrous making. Had I simply come to The Lair, accepting a different approach, I might not have needed the ambrein at all.

It all feels so pointless now. My fucking sex life. So stupid.

Instead, I've not only put my own career in question, I've

pulled my closest friend into this mess. I won't let her take the blame, though. No matter what she says, Price Alexander Wells is mine to claim.

CHAPTER 6

TORN

QUINN

Plundering through Maddox's cases is like trying to sort through a pigsty. A dirty, slimy pigsty. The demented twists he represents and gets off of their charges is gnawing at my stomach. I have to eat nearly half a bottle of antacids just to get through the past three months in PACER. The public access records don't hold all the info I need, but it's a start.

This is why cops have to leave a case once we make a collar. The alternative to see a case through would drive us mad. I feel like I'm halfway there now.

I've somehow managed to make three rows on my board. Maddox's colleagues. Maddox's supervisors. And Maddox's questionable clients. The client column is filling up fast.

When I go in to question the lawyer, I want to know everything about this prick. From when he got his first nut, down to the moment he started running for the Commonwealth's office.

I do all right with the behavioral bit. Enough to put together a decent profile of Maddox. But Sadie would knock it out of the park. She'd have this asshole nailed down before we even approached him.

I exhale a long breath and click a new window open on my laptop. It's my call to bring her back. I know this. But I first need to sort my own bullshit. Working a case like this doesn't leave a lot of time for that.

As if on cue, my phone vibrates in its holder. I unclip it from my belt and open the notification. *187 – Courthouse Metro District*

Son of a bitch.

I grab my coat, quickly putting away my research on Maddox before I head out. My gut says it's another pro. It's in the same general area, which is starting to form a pattern.

Carson's waiting for me at the front of the bullpen. "Am I riding with you?"

In just under two decades, I've had exactly two partners. I learned early on in my rookie detective years that I worked better alone. The first partner moved up quickly through the ranks, making it easy. The second… Well, even before it was official, Sadie was my partner from day one. When you click with someone on a professional level and come to depend on their insight, it just happens naturally.

Regardless of my reservations as to where that partnership stands between us now, I'm not seeking a substitution. Carson's a skilled detective for his age, but he's also a weasel. And no one's weaseling their way into Sadie's spot.

"Take your own car," I say as I walk past.

I glimpse the disappointment on his face and damn. I still have a fucking soft spot for the rookies. "We might need to split up once we get an ID," I add, just to give the guy a break.

"Right," he says, grabbing his keys.

I lead the way there, flipping on my blue and reds without the siren once I pull up to the crime scene. Another alley, another body dump. But this time, the perp didn't bother to try to dispose of the body. I spot the vic from inside my car. Her body tucked closely to the brick wall of the building.

As I head toward the unis yellow-taping the scene, Carson comes up beside me. "Different MO? He didn't discard the body. Maybe this perp wants us to know what he's done."

I shake my head. "Lifting dead weight isn't easy. Even for a strong fucker. Most likely, after the discovery of the first vic, he didn't bother wasting his time or energy."

Carson nods.

Once I reach the vic, I clear out CSU so I can study the scene. White female. Early twenties. Her face shows signs of bruising, as do her wrists and forearms. Not as badly as the first vic; I can make out her features, which hold a hint of an undeterminable ethnicity, and some of the bruises are yellow and fading. Her black dress could be cheap or expensive. I need a woman's perspective on this one. But the vic's hair is highlighted, and her makeup is heavy and smeared.

One black heel is on, the other off. I glance around.

"Looks like we have a Cinderella," Carson says. "I already checked the area. Nothing else in the vicinity linking to the vic."

"Okay, good. See if Avery's on her way. I need a couple of pointers on the wardrobe."

Carson sends a quick text, then says, "Could be a serial rapist. He's not mutilating the vics. Not putting on a show. Not leaving behind any signatures."

"We need COD first," I note. "But you're right. These kills seem to be cause and effect, more out of necessity. We'll know more once the lab can confirm if she was raped."

And I hope Avery can. As sickening as it is chasing a serial rapist, it's a lot easier to stomach than mutilated corpses and copycat serial killers mimicking ancient countesses.

Something neat and straightforward.

I'm directing CSU on processing samples from her bare foot, collecting any trace she might've picked up from the kill site, when I see Avery walking up.

My chest tightens. I have to physically press my hand against my ribs to calm the palpitations.

She sets her kit down and pulls a band from around her wrist to tie her long blond hair back. Even in her shiny lab jacket and cargo pants, her shapely curves are noticeable. My mind wanders, recalling how her short robe inched up to reveal her thighs…and I have to look away.

I'm a fucking mess of a man.

As Avery approaches the scene, her deep brown eyes meet mine. "Detective Quinn."

I flinch at her cool greeting. Before I can address her, she acknowledges Carson and then squats next to the vic to start her examination.

Carson shoots me a curious glare, but he's smart enough not to probe.

This is exactly why you don't cross that damn line with colleagues. If I could go back, I'd kick my ass for even thinking about going to Avery's last night. What did that achieve?

But as I watch Avery work, her swift and sure movements collecting trace and the way she delicately handles the vic, the sadness in her eyes—eyes that have seen too many victims without ever becoming void of emotion—I'm convinced. Avery gives so much of herself to the job, the least I can do is be there when she needs somebody.

"Quinn. Take a look at this."

At her request, I promptly order Carson off to start the canvass of the local establishments, and kneel next to Avery. "You find something interesting?"

"I wasn't sure before…" she says as she lifts the hem of the vic's dress. She pushes it back to reveal the upper thigh. I lean in to get a closer look at what Avery points out beneath the band of the vic's underwear. "I found something similar on the first vic. I thought it was some kind of tattoo in the process of removal. The raised design was badly damaged due to a burn she sustained. But now…seeing it again…"

"It's a brand," I say. And the perp was trying to get rid of the evidence the first time around.

"I'll work up a sketch. I'll match it to what I can determine of the first vic's marking and compare. But they do look similar in design."

"Thanks," I say, taking one last look at the brand before meeting Avery's eyes. "Try to get me that sketch as soon as possible."

Her mouth presses together. "Sure thing."

I jot down notes as Avery records her findings. She describes the dress as designer. I make an additional note to track down where it was purchased.

"I'll need to perform an autopsy to determine cause of death," she says. "There's nothing to indicate she died in a similar manner as the other vic, so I can't conclusively say whether you're looking for the same offender. I'll let you know as soon as I have COD."

As she packs up, I observe her stiff movements. And when she tosses her gloves into her kit with more force than necessary, that pain beats to fucking life in my chest. I wish I could reach in and tear it out.

Knowing I'll probably regret asking, I go in anyway. "What's wrong?"

"Nothing," she clips.

With an internal groan, I cross my arms. "We're not going to get anywhere unless you're honest with me."

Her eyes snap to mine. "Honesty. All right." She clicks her kit closed and stands. "I saw Sadie today."

Avery has a punch like a damn wrecking ball.

"Whatever your hang-up is," she continues. "You need to get over it. We need her working this case."

Speechless, I turn away, trying to collect my thoughts. Within the seconds it takes me to wrap my head around her accusation, Avery is already marching down the alley. Hell. I take off, picking up my pace once I pass the unis.

"Mind elaborating just a bit," I say as I fall into step with her.

"Not really. I think it's pretty straightforward."

She turns the corner around the building, and I'm right behind her. "Stop for a minute."

Surprisingly, she does. She doesn't look at me, but I can tell by the rise and fall of her shoulders that she's upset. I proceed with caution.

"I know you and Sadie are close, but you've never gotten irate over any of my and Sadie's disagreements before. And there's been plenty." When she doesn't respond, I move in front of her. "So is it me? Did I say or do something wrong last night?"

The corner of her mouth hikes. "Men. So vain. Even you, Quinn. If I take issue and call out some bullshit on the job, then it has to be something you've done, right?"

I step toward her, my tone lighter. "But you are calling out the bullshit on me. So yeah, I think it's a logical leap." I can't help the smile twitching at my lips.

Avery's forehead creases, her lips purse. "Well…okay. Anyway. I would just feel better if Sadie were here also."

"Me, too," I admit. This gets a raised eyebrow from her. "But that's beside the point. You're holding something back—something that's eating at you."

"Damn," she mutters. "Anyone ever tell you that human lie detector thing kind of makes you an asshole?"

I smirk. "Only all the time."

Wiping her hand across her forehead, Avery leans her back against the building. She looks up at me. "I think I'm in trouble."

The faces of every guy I've seen her with over the past couple of days flashes before my eyes. I'm mentally beating the shit out of each one, as I demand, "Who is it?"

"What?" She squints. "No. Nothing personal. God, not that." She bites the corner of her bottom lip, and that action does something to me. I draw closer to her, unable to deny the pull. "I would've told you sooner, but I was shaken. I already sent the sample to forensics, though. I'll have more information tomorrow."

"Then just tell me," I say, my patience wearing thin.

She licks her lips, hesitant. "I may've found—no. I *did* find a good amount of ambrein in the vic's system."

My shoulders tense. I get closer, lowering my voice. "Your drug. The one you developed?"

She nods. "I didn't get a chance to analyze it, but I know the compound was mine. Partially, anyway. It had been altered."

"Altered into what?" My hands lock into fists inside my trench coat pockets.

"I don't know." As her eyes search mine, I spot real fear in hers. Not the panicked terror I witnessed in her brown irises that night on The Countess. But the kind of anxiety that makes you question yourself. "All I know is that you were right. I might've inadvertently given the wrong people the cocktail. If these women are connected, and this vic has the same compound in her system…I don't know what it means. But I might know who's responsible, Quinn."

Real fucking fear plows through me. "Have you told anyone else?"

"Just Sadie," she says quickly.

A stab of pain spasms beneath my ribs. I shuffle around my pocket and pull out an empty roll of antacids. "Sadie," I repeat. I need to get ahead of this. If Avery is somehow mixed up with some bad people, I don't need Sadie going all vigilante.

Not again.

"You need to separate yourself from this case," I tell Avery. "Hand it over to someone you trust in the lab. I'll get you a detail of unis until—"

"No."

I close in until I'm near enough to smell the scent of lavender in her shampoo. "I don't tell you how to do your job. Don't tell me how to do mine." I stare down, holding her gaze. "Until I make the connection, and I know you're not in any danger, or can't be implicated…you don't touch this. We're doing this one by the book."

"This one?" Her voice is soft, questioning. But her eyes drill right into me.

Damn. I don't make these kind of mistakes. Only here recently, and only now more and more when Avery's involved. My control is being tested. Like now, as she cocks her head back challengingly. Daring me with the truth.

My jaw tightens. "Don't make me be an asshole, Avery. If I have to get you removed from the crime lab, if that's what it takes to protect you, then that's what I'll do."

Her eyes narrow. "You need me," she says.

Against my will, my body responds, my arms bracketing either side of her body. "I need you safe—"

"You need the answers I have. I'm the only one who can tell you how the drug was altered. I'm the only one who knows my formula. And I might not have names, but I have locations. I can put together a sting—"

I clasp her chin. "Like hell. You'll give me everything you know and I'll handle it. The less you're involved, the better."

Her gaze slits into a glare, but she doesn't pull away from my touch. My fingers burn where we connect. "You don't trust me."

"This has nothing to do with trust," I say, enforcing conviction into my tone. Regardless of any suspicion I harbor about the last case, what I suspect of Sadie's involvement, or what I assume Avery may know…the truth of the matter is Avery's safety.

"You've been through enough already," I add. "It's best if I take care—"

She scoffs. "That's it, then. Fragile Avery. I don't need to be sheltered, Quinn." She windmills her forearm, breaking out of my hold, but I grip her shoulders and keep her against the wall.

"You don't want to be treated like a victim, then stop acting like one. You're smarter than this. You know protocol, you know procedure, and you're *not* fragile. But you will damn sure get yourself into deep shit trying to prove it like this."

She blinks. "You don't see me as a victim," she says, the question in that statement clear.

"No. I don't."

Her hand snakes up to rest on my chest. My heart pounds, beating the fuck out of my rib cage as she leans into me, her sultry mouth just inches from mine. "Then prove it. Prove that you don't think I'll break if you touch me—*really* touch me."

Her body heat presses against me, and it's torture. I watch her mouth part, her tongue trace her teeth, tempting me closer. My hands grip her arms to hold her back, but I could just as easily pull her to me. And I almost do…

"That won't prove anything, Avery," I say, forcing myself to release her. "Other than I'd be a bastard for taking advantage of…the situation."

She mock laughs. "And what situation is that? My poor, delicate mental state?" She shakes her head. "Saint Quinn. Always doing what's right." She steps around me, but pauses near to whisper, "But just think how much fun it would be if you relinquished that righteous control of yours."

I plant my hands against the wall, my fingers digging into the brick. My teeth grit until my jaw aches as I let her walk away. Then I take the long way back around the building toward the crime scene, allowing my aching balls to walk off the shame.

CHAPTER 7

WARNING

AVERY

I'm no detective, but I have enough conviction to make up for what I lack in the sleuthing department. After I uploaded the pic I took of the victim's thigh at the crime scene, I initiated an online image scan, determined to match the brand.

So far, nothing remotely close. It's not as if there's a criminal social network where victims' pics are traded like baseball cards. Not on the Internet I can access at work, anyway. I'll have to dive deeper later, once I'm at home and on my own personal interface. But as it is, Quinn will probably have more luck searching the police databases than I will on the darknet.

At least I was able to confirm that the partial brand on the first vic is in fact the same design branded on the second. That links the two victims together. There's a connection there, but of what...I have no idea.

Once I forwarded the sketch to Quinn, I sent the interns home. Needing this space to myself to conduct my experiment. I could go home, but I feel safer in the same building as Quinn—even if this lab is now tainted.

I groan and close my laptop, angry with myself for letting Quinn effect me. Doesn't he realize this is all I have? That if he shuts me out, I'll go crazy just sitting at home, watching reruns. There're only so many episodes of *Grey's Anatomy* a pathologist can watch before you start questioning your sanity.

And I can't do that again. I can't sit back and wait, wondering what the next step is. This time, I'm calling the shots. I'm not sure what happens now, but I know my part: getting to the bottom of the altered cocktail. That's one area where I know exactly what I'm doing.

I hurriedly change clothes; trading out my field pants for the black maxi skirt I wore in to work, then slip on my lab coat, ready to move ahead with the comparison testing.

As I distribute samples of the ambrein compound into two dishes, I can't stop thinking about how Quinn pulled the same shit with Sadie. It's like he's on some misogynistic kick with the women in his department. Hell, I'm not even *in* his department, and yet he feels he has control over my career. *Control freak.*

I push away from my desk, frustrated. And immediately, remorse seizes my mood. Quinn is a lot of things—a stubborn control freak being at the top of the list—but he's not sexist, and he's not on my case because he thinks I can't handle the job. I get it. If I were in his position, I'd have sent any lab tech home instantly.

Especially if that tech started coming on to me…

Mortified, I bury my face in my hands. *What the hell is wrong with me*?

He must think I've lost it. That I've officially lost my freaking mind. If he didn't have a good reason to have me removed from this case before, I just gave him one.

A *bang* sounds from the main lab, and I flinch.

The body. Right.

Completely lost in thought, I forgot Carson sent notice that they were wrapping up at the crime scene and vic number two was on her way here. I stand and smooth my palms down my lab coat before exiting my office. As soon as I see the two transfer crewmembers wheeling the stretcher through the double doors, I stop short.

"Where's Derik?" I ask.

Neither answers as they continue to push the stretcher toward the middle of the lab. I take a step back. Their gaze is aimed at the floor, their faces hidden behind the bill of their baseball hats, and something just isn't…right.

I've been overly paranoid since returning to work. Which I assumed was normal. I was bound and gagged and tortured in this very room...before I was stolen away by the monster. I had to rationalize my fears before I could even step foot back inside the lab. But after the discovery of the ambrein, that paranoia feels amplified.

Why did I think I could ever be here alone?

I slip a hand inside my coat pocket and wrap sweaty fingers around the Mace clipped to my key ring. The one Quinn gave me—a first day back on the job present. At the time, I didn't appreciate the reminder. But now, I'm thankful. Paranoid or not, I'm prepared.

One of the crewmembers looks up and smiles. "Derik called in sick today. We're filling in." He unhooks a clipboard from the stretcher and holds it out to me.

With a shaky exhale, I release the Mace. *I can't live in fear.*

Accepting the clipboard, I sign my name on the paperwork. When I glance up to hand it back, the guy's smile morphs into a sneer. There's only a second for panic to set in before something covers my face.

Fight-or-flight adrenaline surges, and it's fight that kicks in first. Pen still gripped in my fist, I thrust downward and connect with the man's thigh behind me. An angry growl roars in the shell of my ear, my eardrum crackling with the force of it.

"The bitch stabbed me!"

The black bag covering my head cinches tight around my neck. My hands go to my throat. I try to pry my fingers between the bag and my neck before fear grips my senses. Arms surround me, and I'm lifted in the air.

I hit the floor hard, releasing a strangled cry as pain bites into my back.

Pressure bears down on me as one of the men straddles my chest. My air supply is pinched off, my hands pulled over my head. The Mace long forgotten.

"Someone wants a word with you, bitch," the guy on top of me says.

The material molds to my open mouth as I gulp in hot breaths. I blink rapidly, struggling to get a visual of my attackers through the cloth, but the pitch black only terrifies me more every time I open my eyes.

I squeeze them closed, focus on the sounds.

The swing of the double doors, then heavy footfalls. Slow, deliberate. Somehow that measured patience—as if this person has all the time in the world—scares me the most.

My muscles tense as I thrash against his hold on my arms. It's useless—but I'm not giving up. Not this time.

"Hello, Doctor Johnson."

The man's voice booms, deep and calm. I don't recognize it.

"I apologize for this less than cordial meeting, but my time is precious. And I'm running short on it."

I work words past the burn choking my throat. "What do you want?"

"Seeing how I'm here, taking a great risk to meet with you when I could've just snatched you from anywhere, I gather you can imagine. You're quite intelligent, Miss Johnson."

I try to shake my head, but my stretched arms interfere with any movement. "I can't imagine. Who are you?"

He chuckles. "You had little qualms about fabricating evidence for a mutual acquaintance's unfortunate death." A beat. "So, I come to you now with the same request. Well, request isn't quite right. *Demand* is more appropriate."

The weight crushing my chest is suddenly gone as I'm yanked upright. I hear a *pop* in my shoulder, and blinding white pain shoots across my blacked-out vision.

"Gently, please. Doctor Johnson mustn't be harmed," the man instructs his thugs.

Shoulder throbbing, I'm guided toward a table where I'm forcefully seated on a stool. "I can't just change my findings like that. It has to be supported by the evidence. It has to be believable." It's like someone else is speaking through me; or the fright has vanished. At one point with Wells, I no longer shook when he made threats.

I'm not accepting my fate—just the opposite. But pleading for my life, begging not to be harmed…it doesn't work. These men will do what they've come here to do, regardless. My only power is in keeping my mind sharp.

With what wits I have, I try not to flinch when something is set on the table before me.

"My associate is going to remove the bag now," the man says. "Don't make the mistake of turning around, Miss Johnson." I feel him brush against my back, then his hand clasps my neck. I recoil, my breaths coming faster. His finger skims my lips through the material. "I, unlike our mutual friend, take no pleasure in the suffering of women," he whispers near my ear. "Your death will be quick."

I believe him.

I nod my answer.

The bag is yanked away, and I blink my vision clear. My head trembles, matching the quake rolling through my body as I strain to keep from turning my head.

"Locate the reports on the recently deceased and conclude that the first woman, our dear Miss Beloff, you deem an accident. And then do the same for Miss Carter."

I look down at the table. My laptop. "I haven't even performed the autopsy on the second victim yet," I say, assuming Miss Carter is who has just been brought in.

"That's why I've made this special trip. I'm here to fill in the gaps and help you. I'm giving you the information you need. Both deaths *were* an accident." He *tsks*. "Such a shame, too. I assure you, it was not my desire for them to die. Quite the opposite."

Anger lashes through me like a whip. "The severe beating Marcy Beloff took would suggest otherwise."

My head is wrenched back as he grips a fistful of my hair. His fingers dig at my scalp…and as his nails break skin, I pray he's leaving behind DNA.

"I hope there's not going to be a problem with my request." His hot words sting the side of my face. "Because if pleasantries don't persuade your cooperation, then I assure you, I have other ways."

His hand tightens in my hair, preventing me from turning in either direction, as his body draws closer. "Maybe you're damaged, Miss Johnson. Could it be that after our friend Wells treated you so abhorrently, you now only respond to violence?"

The press of something hard and heavy touches my leg.

My whole body freezes. The air in my lungs, the tremble of my limbs stops—I'm petrified.

I don't like guns. I've worked within the criminal justice field for years and, up until recently, have never had the need for one. Even after I was held captive by a sadistic serial killer, I was never tempted to own a gun.

The cold steel of the barrel assaults my skin as the gun digs under the hem of my skirt. It inches higher, dragging my skirt with it, and I find my voice. "Please…don't."

The weapon comes to a stop at my inner thigh. "I don't revel in suffering, Miss Johnson," he says. "But I've had to do many tasteless things in my past. And it's just like riding a bike; you don't forget."

Within the same moment I swallow my yelp, the barrel is lodged beneath my underwear and bites into the tender flesh of my core. My whole body comes alive with an uncontrollable tremor. Hysteria pulls me under, sucking my mind into a black undertow, void of this abstract reality.

"Stay with me, Avery," he orders, my name sounding too intimate. He holds the gun steady just inside me, a violation of an even more intimate nature as he issues another command. "Now type."

I place a shaky hand on top of my laptop. A thousand questions rush me through the fear. All of which I'm sure will end my life if I'm given the answers. Do I want to know how this man knows about Wells—the monstrous things he did to me; how I forged his COD report—badly enough to die for?

I crack the laptop. Log in to my interface and open the reports. As I type, the barrel of the gun ensures I make no other movement. I finish editing the cause of death for the first victim, citing that further tests prove the damage she sustained to her liver was determined to be accidental. Then, barely finding my voice, I ask, "How did Miss Carter die?"

I use her name instead of thinking of her as a numbered victim, hoping that enforcing the fact she was a person will nudge the humanity in this man.

"Once you autopsied her, you'd have discovered a common denominator between the two women." His voice is low, too close, and I don't mistake his use of the past tense. I still my breathing, the feel of the gun more threatening with every breath. "We're calling it Trifecta. You know it better as your ambrein cocktail, but our batch has far more kick."

I wince. "They died because of me?"

His laugh is dark and disturbing. "No, Miss Johnson. Ease your mind. We've got our own cooks, who did a fine job of improving your mix, though we did need it for the base. That was essential. However, as you can see, we've run into some minor…setbacks."

Death is a *minor* setback? "You can't just use people like lab rats," I say, disgust evident in my tone.

He chuckles again, and the weight of the gun assaults me. "See? You are smart. You're putting the pieces together. But you're not in a position to pass judgment, Miss Johnson." The pressure increases between my thighs, and my stomach pitches with nausea. I stare at the laptop screen, trying to glimpse his reflection. The only thing I can make out is the crest on his necktie: the initials AK.

"Complete Miss Carter's report stating she overdosed on painkillers. You'll find opioids in her system. A suicide or accident, if you will. Whichever you believe is more likely in these circumstances."

I swallow hard as I type my notes into the report. This won't matter. The reports can be overridden. Not by me…I won't make it out of this alive—I know this. But Quinn won't accept my findings. There are too many other factors linking these two deaths together. The brand on the victims' thighs, for one. He'll question the reports. He won't let it go. And once I'm found dead…

Quinn won't stop until he has the truth.

I run my finger over the base of the laptop; a message to Quinn. Because I believe he won't give up.

As I log the last statement, the man beside me sighs. And the gun is suddenly removed. As the steel leaves my body, I slump forward and gasp in full breaths. With trembling hands, I grip my skirt, clinging to it as I force it down my legs.

"Thank you for being so cooperative, Doctor Johnson," he says as he backs away. "Now, it'd be wise for your cooperation to continue as we move on to the next phase."

I close my eyes, wrapping my arms around my stomach as I shrink onto the stool. "I've done all I can do. I can't help you any further."

Hands clamp my arms and I'm hauled backward. Before the scream makes it past my throat, tape is slapped over my mouth. The bag swiftly covers my face once again. I struggle against the brutes, but my hands are pulled behind my back and my wrists fastened with a zip tie before I raise a fist.

One of them yanks my hair, snapping my head back. I feel the intense presence of the man slink near me. "I thought you'd continue your great deducing skills, Miss Johnson," he says close to my ear, his hand brushing my cheek through the cloth and making me shiver. "Of course you can help me further. And you will."

My only prayer as I'm dragged from the lab is that Quinn checks the surveillance in time. That these assholes don't have the skills Wells did to pull off a clean abduction—that they've made a mistake. But as I'm thrown into the back of the transport van, I know my prayer is useless.

These men are nothing like Wells. Wells was the parasite feasting on the bottom rung. And these men… They are the monsters at the top of the food chain.

CHAPTER 8

PURSUE

QUINN

"Contact me right away if you get a hit on anything close to a match," I tell the tech analyst.

He starts the search, hitting the precinct and national databases at the same time. With any luck, we'll find other working girls carrying the same brand. Preferably alive. Not that questioning a pro has ever produced much in the way of aiding in any investigation, but it could give us a clue as to what we're dealing with.

I save a new copy of the scanned image Avery texted to my phone. My thumbs hover over the onscreen keyboard. I type out "thank you" and hit Send before I close out the text.

What else can I say? Thanks for the blue balls? Thanks for making me feel like the shittiest man alive?

Better to let this one simmer.

I'm aware that I'm avoiding the bigger issue between us,

but being married to a pissed off woman has taught me when to tuck balls and duck. There's nothing I can say to Avery that won't come out wrong, come back to bite me. She needs more time…and I need to solve this case before another girl winds up dead in my city.

The thought of announcing another serial killing spree to the media turns my stomach. But one more body, and that's what we'll have.

My next logical course is to get the dirt on Maddox. Find out his connection to the first vic. I need an ID on the second girl to establish a link to both vics through Maddox, then I'll have enough to bring him in for questioning.

No reason to spook the lawyer until I can build a case showing he's good for this. Sadie would advise not to focus on one lead, to look at more than one perp. Which is what I should be doing, but I just feel this one in my gut. If Maddox isn't our guy, then he damn well knows who is. He's connected to this somehow.

As I grab the printouts I made of Maddox's past cases off my desk, my phone beeps.

I look down at the screen: *503 – white van – last seen Arl Blvd*

Why am I getting pinged with an auto theft? I put a call in to Carson. He picks up on the first ring. "Where are you?"

Static from the radio crackles in the background. "I'm in pursuit. Two unis radioed in an attack on the bus from the crime scene. It was hijacked."

A cold blast of fear slaps my face. "And the driver?"

"He's alive, but doesn't know much. He reported two perps."

"Do you have eyes on the bus?" I ask, my feet already taking me out of my office.

"Negative. It went off the grid. I know it's not my call, but I was in the vicinity. I figured our vic's on that bus."

"Good call, Carson." I point to two unis as I make my way through the bullpen. "That stolen transport van; I want all updates as soon as they come in," I say to them. Then to Carson: "Keep me posted."

"What are you thinking?" he asks, catching me off-guard before I hang up.

I blow out a tense breath. Ever since Avery's confession, I've been racking my brain on how to use the information she has while still keeping her safe. I know damn well that some petty car thief didn't steal that transport van. But why try to hide evidence now? Why not burn the body or toss it into the river beforehand?

Regardless, this case just escalated. And until I know just who and what is involved…Avery's not safe.

The roiling knot twisting my gut has never steered me wrong, but— "Could be two idiots picked the wrong damn van to steal. They'll end up on some dumbest criminal show for hijacking a dead body."

Carson's laugh lightens my mood some. "So you're going back to the scene?"

"No," I say, passing the bank of elevators and taking the stairs, impatient to see Avery. "M.E. lab."

Silence stretches out over the line, and I hate that he's picked up on my train of thought. Which I need contradicted. Now. "Just get a visual on that bus, Carson. And drive safe."

"You're worried about me, Detective Quinn. That' so—"

"Shut it, Carson. Do your job."

"Yes, sir. On it," he confirms.

I end the call as I reach the hallway. The deathly quiet that fills this floor has always been unsettling, but as I push through the swing doors, that stagnant stillness grips my spine with icy fingers.

"Avery—" I shout, her name a mocking echo in the empty lab.

My chest tight, I head straight for her office. Without conscious effort, I take in the scene. The lights are on, her laptop left out in the open, a stool overturned…and a body on a stretcher.

"Shit." I pause long enough at the stretcher to confirm it's the same vic from the crime scene. My heart thunders as I take off toward her office. I yank the door open. She's not here. And she wouldn't just leave her office unlocked.

I pull my cell out and click her name. The call goes right to voicemail. "Fuck."

Fuck!

I call Carson, my question ready as soon as he picks up. "How do you know the vic is on that bus?"

His response is immediate. "The driver was attacked right after he left the scene. It was a pretty good assumption, but—why?"

"The body's at the lab." I grip the phone, my whole body tense.

"Car thieves making body deliveries to the precinct?" Carson tries to reason, sounding just as lost as I feel.

I cut him off before he can continue that thought. "I want that bus found."

"GPS is still down—"

"Get the fucking techs to hack it," I roar.

A moment passes, then: "Quinn, where's Avery?" Carson asks.

I close my eyes, my breath sawing in and out of my constricted lungs. "I don't know, but I'm going to find her." Then I hang up before I lose my shit for fucking certain.

When's the last time anyone saw her?

I click Sadie's number with the weight of an anvil in my gut. Getting a grip on the climbing panic, I tell myself these two are as thick as thieves lately. Avery probably took off from the crime scene, pissed at me. She never even came back to the lab. She went to Sadie, needing someone to commiserate with. Hell, they can bash me and call me an asshole all day long…

just as long as Avery's safe.

When Sadie's throaty voice answers, I swallow my pride. "Bonds, tell me you know where Avery is."

Time seems to freeze as I wait to hear her confirm my theory. "Quinn, no. She's not with me. Have you tried the lab?"

My fist connects with the wall. I grit my teeth as pain slices through my knuckles. But it's nothing compared to the fear tearing me open from the inside.

"Quinn, what's wrong? What's going on?" Sadie asks, barely masking her concern.

The hitch of alarm in her voice steals the last of my clinging hope. "Avery may've gotten into something over her head. I need you to try to find her while I track her phone." Do I put out an APB? Wexler will have my ass if she's just sitting at home, ignoring my calls. But as I look around the lab, deja vu in the worst way crashes over me.

I wasn't in time to save her before.

Every second counts. Deciding I'm not taking any chances with Avery's life, I say, "Bonds, you check her house. I'm putting out an APB and then I'll get a trace on her last location—"

"I'm coming with you," Sadie says, her no argument tone clear. "Colton can check all her usual haunts. We'll find her, Quinn."

The reassurance in her voice overrides the brimming irritation at hearing his name. I don't want that guy anywhere near this, but there's no time to debate. Avery comes first.

"Meet me at the lab," I say and end the call, my mind already processing the scene.

Jesus. Why the hell would she be alone? She was abducted from this very fucking spot before—but that was different. Simon had access to her. He was her own damn lab tech. And maybe that's it; she feels safer working on her own. Pushing the facts of what she suffered at the hands of Simon from my mind, I focus on the evidence here.

I slide the body hanger over with too much force, nearly ripping it from the wall. "Where is she?" I shout. The vic lies lifeless on the stretcher, the only witness.

I'm reliving Avery's abduction all over again, only this time, I'm too close. And I'm not helping Avery by getting in my own way. Gaining a shred of composure, I radio in to the tech working on the search. "Jason. I need you to go through the M.E. lab security footage right away. I want as many eyes on it as possible."

"Ten-four," he replies.

My adrenaline soars. *Focus.* If anything happens to Avery… I can't go there. Not yet. I make one last call to CSU and order a rush on processing the lab. This has to be done right.

I hope I'm wrong. For fuck's sake, I pray Avery is at some dive bar drinking her bitter resentment at me away. I'll take the hit from Wexler gladly if that's the case.

Starting at the top, I trace my steps back to the double

doors and slip on a pair of gloves, making sure I cover the blood on my knuckles. I fumble for a loose marker I put in my pocket at the crime scene and drop it by the doors.

When I reach the table with the overturned stool, I open the laptop. The screen blinks on, a passcode barring me access. I brace the heels of my hands against the table, my gaze hard on the screen. Then, I see it.

My chest ignites in a fiery ache.

I push off the table and search for print powder. *Dammit. Where does she keep it*? I locate it in a drawer and rush back to the table. With less than steady hands, I dust the brush lightly over the lower part of the laptop, right below the keyboard.

The white powder begins to reveal the message, but I already know what it reads before I reach the last letter: HELP

A message from Avery. As she sat here knowing some fate was about to befall her.

My heart rockets to my throat, and the jar of powder careens against the wall as I release a roar.

"That's not going to help her."

My chest heaves. I close my eyes—just for one second—before I turn to face Sadie. "I fucking let this happen. Again."

She might be tiny, but there's nothing inferior about her as she holds me in her perceptive gaze. Sadie fills the room with a determined presence, balancing out the loss of control I feel right this moment.

She pushes the sleeves of her jacket up. "It's not your fault,

Quinn."

She's dead wrong. I should've protected Avery. Even if that meant throwing her over my shoulder again and locking her up in my office. This time, it was within my power, and I pussied out. All because Avery tested my control. Regardless of whatever is skewing my perception of right and wrong…I knew what I was supposed to do, and I fucked up.

Fate's a devious bitch. Toying with her twice so close together…Avery could lose this round. I might not get her back.

"Wherever your brooding thoughts are going," Sadie says, snapping me back to the moment. "Stop." Our eyes meet, and she nails me with a fierce look. "What do we know?"

And like that, she reels me in. My instincts sharpen on the case. When it comes to the job, Sadie's my better half.

"Did Avery tell you anything about the drug—?"

"Yes," she says, heading me off.

Right. Thick as thieves. I nod, walking a circle around the table as CSU enters and immediately starts the sweep.

I give them explicit instructions, directing them to collect all trace from the vic, which is a complicated call to make. Wanting the evidence to be compromised for Avery's sake, means that anything we find—any prior trace that existed before the two perps handled the body—might not hold up in court where the victim is concerned.

My consolation is in knowing that the perps who might

have Avery are connected to the vic's offender. When we save Avery…when we bring in the perps, we're also bringing in the same fuckers who are connected to these deaths.

I walk Sadie through the crime scene, getting her thoughts on the timeline and method. No obvious signs indicate that Avery was hurt, but that only lessons the pressure on my chest a fraction. When this is over, I might just burn this damn lab down. Move Avery into the precinct upstairs and put a damn tracking device on her.

As the CSU team gets to work fingerprinting surfaces, I take a call from upstairs. The security footage cut off over an hour ago, but right before, the transport van was seen on camera pulling into the parking lot.

"She's in that van," I say, turning toward Sadie. "Or she was at least an hour ago. I can't just stand here, waiting…" I ball my hands into fists and curse. "I'm going to find her."

Sadie's by my side as I exit the lab. I put the call in to Wexler, upgrading the scanner alert on the bus to include a law enforcement member aboard, which will ensure a safe recovery of the van, then I get a location on Carson.

The van is still off the grid, but the rookie made the right call. I have a new respect for Carson's instincts.

As I duck into my Crown Vic, I glance over at Sadie climbing into the passenger-seat. "When I find these fuckers this time…" I say, letting my intentions trail off.

But Sadie is right there to pick up what I won't voice. "We

end the threat."

Our gazes lock, and in the private restrains of the car, I don't correct her.

I may still have issues with Sadie's past, with reconciling her actions—but this we agree on.

And that realization terrifies the fuck out of me.

CHAPTER 9

UNDER THE INFLUENCE

AVERY

The windowless room is freezing. Florescent lights hum, echoing off the cinderblock walls and tingeing the too bright, barren room in a sickly green hue. As soon as I was removed from the van and ushered inside, the bag was removed from my head and my lab coat was taken.

The thin blouse I'm left with does nothing to shield me from the frigid air.

I rub my arms to generate heat, giving myself something to concentrate on besides counting the seconds. I've only been locked inside for minutes, but panic threatens to pull me under when I imagine it turning into days.

No. Don't go there.

I'm not shackled. I'm not drugged. So very different than

before, but somehow just as terrifying. Logically, I don't think these people have the same intentions as my abductor did when he took me, but that only serves to frighten me more. The not knowing.

I can still feel the steel of the gun pressed inside me, and I start to pace, keeping myself sane. I can't stop thinking. I want my mind to stop.

Right when I think I'm going to lose it and start banging on the rusted door, I hear a *click*, and the door grinds open against the floor.

The man entering is tall and thickly built. He wears a mask. A Jason mask like on the horror movie. And he's carrying an assault rifle. My stomach plunges, free-fall. I want the bag back over my head.

He jerks his head. "Move. It's ready."

What's ready? But the courage to ask is lost. He doesn't manhandle me, and somehow my feet move me in that direction. I've simply lost my mind. Days, hours, minutes—I've wasted so much time fearing the world after I was released from the hospital. And what I dreaded could happen—that which I told myself over and over would never happen again—has happened.

What else is there left to fear?

Death?

I'm almost relieved. Like I'm ready to welcome it. Like I can stop fearing it now.

The masked man stands in the doorway as I cross through. My eyes go wide when I see what's on the other side of the room.

A lab.

But unlike any lab I've ever worked in. It's dirty and smells of death. Not like the death in the morgue, where I'm accustomed to being surrounded by bodies. But a grotesque, sour stench that soaks my pores.

Tables are full of beakers and test tubes. A giant syringe station is setup with thin blue hoses curling down into a large tub. My gaze follows their path along the back wall to a large containment unit.

"Welcome, Doctor Johnson."

I whirl around, trying to locate the source of the gravelly voice. That familiar voice that raises bile to my throat, remembering the feel of the gun.

Feedback pierces the air, and I look up to find a speaker in the corner.

The voice booms through the room again. "Go ahead. Get comfortable. There's a smock on the hanger to your left, and goggles on the table."

I shake my head. "What do you want from me?" I say to the room, hoping this unsettling PA system is two-way.

"It's what we both want," the voice responds. "I believe neither of us want any more dead girls littering our beautiful streets. So you should get to work."

I turn around and see the man with the gun standing watch at the only exit.

I face forward, lick my lips. "And if I can't?"

The silence stretches out, endlessly taunting. I'm sure the decision to end my life has already been made. Then: "I really don't think that's an option for you, Miss Johnson." A beat. "Best focus on the task at hand. You have one hour."

I glance up above the lab station at an old clock. The secondhand ticking down.

Quinn, find me.

With no other alternative, I approach the table aligned against the wall and find a box of disposable gloves. As I'm sliding on a pair, my eyes flit to the trashcan and my stomach roils with revulsion. Blood doesn't faze me. I'm elbows deep in it most days. But this blood—the blood coating hundreds of pairs of gloves and gauze—is not from the deceased.

This is the blood of the living. The tortured. The tested and experimented on.

The women who—just as I was—are at the mercy of a sadistic monster.

I set to work analyzing the drug, putting the countdown and the women out of my mind. This is my area. I can do this. I just can't think of the consequences once I do…

Surprisingly, the lab is well equipped for what they're trying to achieve. All the chemicals and compounds that are nearly impossible for me to attain are readily available. And in large supply.

When I spot the independent variable, a nauseous tumble rocks my stomach. The drug compound that I notice in analysis right away is one that I would never mix with this cocktail.

Pharmaceutically enhanced MDMA.

Not the run-of-the-mill street drug that, once cut and packaged, is referred to as molly or ecstasy. No. This is pure and concentrated.

This is deadly.

I reach up and adjust my mask, fearful of any powder sneaking past.

"Forty-five minutes, Doctor Johnson." The voice startles me, killing my concentration.

"Dammit," I curse. Centering myself, I prepare my workstation.

I understand what they want. And God help me, I think I know how to give it to them.

Swirling the beaker, I help along the blending of the cocktail. Thin wisps of deep blue coil and bloom out within the clear liquid, tingeing the concoction a bright baby blue. I carefully insert a syringe into the mix.

"It's done," I say, my hands clammy, my face glazed in cold

sweat.

Slow applause performed by one erupts from the speaker. "Very good. I never had any doubt."

I set the filled syringe on the table and tear off my gloves. "I've done as you asked. I corrected the serum. Now I want to be released." My words are bold, much bolder than I feel; exerting a forced bravado that I pray doesn't get me killed.

"Not yet," the man from the PA system says.

I spin around. He now stands in the room, his presence more threatening than the man next to him wielding the assault rifle. His face is hidden behind a featureless, white mask. Somehow, the lack of definition is more terrifying than the horror mask his lackey dons.

"I promise you," I say, straining to remove any quake from my voice, "it's complete. It will work."

He tilts his head. "I have no fear that you believe that, Miss Johnson. But as a doctor, as a scientist, you must know that all experiments have to be tested conclusively."

A whimper directs my attention to another one of his brutes as a woman is thrust into the room. She's clad only in her underwear and bra. Her sleek dark hair mussed, her beautiful face pinched in fear and smeared with makeup as tears track her cheeks.

"No," I say, shaking my head resolutely. "I've done everything you've asked of me. And I promise, my skills surpass whoever formulated this drug before. It will…get the results you want." I cringe, wishing I could detach myself from this reality. "But I won't be party to inflicting this torture on another human. On another woman."

I will die before I become anything comparable to the man who tortured me.

"Brave words." He stalks closer to me. "But I'm afraid this isn't your choice."

The brute of a man anchors an arm around her waist, eliciting a shriek from the traumatized woman. She struggles against his hold, but I can tell she's already too weak, too drained from whatever she's already suffered. Her fight dies too quickly.

The arrogant man before me slinks closer—so close that my trembling physically hurts; my muscles ache as I refrain from looking up to meet his eyes behind the mask. His hand snakes out and grabs the syringe. I flinch.

"Relax, Miss Johnson." He runs a finger along my face, and I recoil. "This will be over quickly."

He turns toward the woman, and before I realize I've reacted, I lunge for his hand. Something wild takes over me, demanding and crazed. "You can't do this to her!"

Within seconds, the man with the gun has me restrained, the barrel pressed against my temple. The hard steel bites into my skin as a sickness washes over me.

This is it. It's all over.

At least I tried.

The man with the white mask faces me. He *tsks*. "Very well, Miss Johnson. I will honor your request, since you've been such an asset thus far."

Relief floods me. Whatever happens next…I can get through it.

Only just as I grasp on to that fleeting ray of hope, it's shattered.

I don't even have time to fight. It happens so suddenly; the man is beside me; the syringe lowered; the needle inserted into my arm. Fire shoots into my system, racing through my bloodstream. My vision flickers as heat blankets my skin.

As my muscles go lax, I wilt against the strong arms supporting me. My head lulls against his hard chest.

"I expect we'll get much better results from you, anyway," he says, dropping the syringe in the trash and wiping his hands off on his slacks. "What better test subject than the drug designer herself?"

A dizziness sweeps over my senses, and I shake my head. The room spins. "I want…to leave."

He chuckles. "Of course. We can't very well record your progress here, can we?" He aims his attention to the man holding me at gunpoint. "Relocate her. *Securely*," he stresses. "After all, the boss should be the one to enjoy the fruits of our accomplishment."

It's right on the tip of my tongue…the question. Wanting to know who this illusive *boss* is. But like the woman to my left, my fight has evaporated. As the drug blasts my arteries, exploding in euphoric shivers over my body…I'm lost.

My last thought: *Quinn, save me.*

CHAPTER 10

CONTROL

QUINN

"GPS has just been triggered on the bus."

I hear Carson's update, but I'm too invested in my rage for it to register.

"Quinn." Sadie's voice bleeds through the radio static. She reaches for the handset. "Carson, what's the location?"

"Last pinged heading east toward TRM Bridge," he responds.

That does sink in. Avery's being taken to DC. Across the state line and into another jurisdiction. *Not happening.*

I check my rearview right before I pull off onto the median and come to an abrupt stop. Sadie braces her hands on the dash and swears. We're moving again, making a hard U-turn before she has the chance to reprimand me.

"Hell, Quinn..."

Hell isn't here—not today. If I have any say, Avery's slipping right through its clutches. I'm driving toward oncoming traffic, cars blaring horns and veering left out of the way, until I find a clear space in the median to cross over.

We hit the patch of grass with a hard bump, another curse from Sadie, and I swerve into the right lane.

"We're going to save her," Sadie assures. "But not if you kill us first."

My mouth crooks into a smile. "This from the woman who set off on her own to face a serial killer?"

I can't see it, but I can *feel* her scowl. Those narrowed green eyes drilling me. "I thought we weren't ever going to mention it."

I pass a car, shooting around to get ahead of traffic. I grunt my derision. "I'm not mentioning *it*...technically. I'm expressing my dislike for your carelessness."

I peek over to see her eyebrows hike. "Expressing, huh. Since when does hardboiled Detective Ethan Quinn express himself?" Her laugh is clipped. "What the hell's gotten into you?"

Ignoring the baiting comment, I focus on getting through the intersection before the yellow light turns red.

"Carson," Sadie says into the handset. "We need an update."

A hiss of static. "Still eastbound on GWM and coming up on the island. I'm ten minutes away."

"We're less than one," she says, planting her hand on the

dash to prepare for the sharp turn up ahead. "Notify all unis for backup. We're in pursuit."

I take the turn, feeling the tires lose traction with the road. Gripping the wheel tighter, I pull the car straight and punch the gas. Then I lock onto it. The transport van is making time in traffic, doing the speed limit. Trying to go undetected.

You're fucking detected.

Thanks to the brains in the department, they were able to override the disabled GPS system on the bus. And now we're close.

She's close. I can feel it. Still, the fucking ache in my chest won't stop until I see her inside the van…alive.

I reach for the controls and shut off the siren, but it's too late. The bus guns it.

"Shit." A stealth attack is lost. Time to improvise.

"Find something and hang on," I advise Sadie.

Pulling up beside the Audi directly behind the bus, I honk. The driver looks over, a pissed off expression on his face, until he sees the flashing blue and reds. I flip on the siren, and his car slows to a crawl, getting annoyed honks from the cars piling up behind.

I snag the radio. "I need a stretch of GWM cleared up ahead, Carson. Make it happen."

"I got you," he replies.

I hope he does.

The bus picks up speed. I stay on its tail, keeping at a safe distance. We need to stop it before it reaches a dangerous speed.

"Bonds. Shoot the back tire out."

With another cop, I might get a shocked retort. A complaint about filling out paperwork for discharging their weapon. And I wouldn't ask anyone that I didn't trust to pull it off while keeping Avery safe.

That's exactly why I ask her.

Sadie doesn't hesitate. She unbuckles her seatbelt and unclips her SIG from the holster. I lower the window for her as she peels off her jean jacket.

"Aim low," I say.

Gaze straight ahead, she says, "I'm good."

Angling her body halfway out the window, she tests her balance. She keeps her gun out of sight until I'm close enough. Then she hunkers near the side-view mirror and aims.

Pop. Pop.

Two blasts. One from her gun, the other from the tire blowout.

The van zigzags with a screech as the driver tries to regain control. I veer off to the left, coming up beside the bus to help guide it onto the median. The driver puts up a fight at first, but I nudge him—not so lightly—with the side of the Crown Vic and he relents.

He knows he's through; he's not making an escape on a flat.

I'm already pulling my gun once I'm parked ahead of the van. "Stay here—" I say, but Sadie's opening the door before I can finish. "Shit."

I jump out and round the car, gun aimed. "Hands on the wheel! Hands on the wheel! Let me see them."

Adrenaline soars. My roaring blood pulses in my ears as I get a lock on the driver. From my peripheral, I glimpse Sadie mirroring my stance, gun drawn and ready to fire at any threat.

My gaze snags the man's hands as he eases them onto the wheel. Slowly, I move in.

And I see her.

Avery's there, her face just visible through the grate divider.

My relief is so strong, I damn near buckle at the knees. But I check myself, churning the residual anger still brimming at the surface into a weapon. I order the perp to keep his hands raised and slowly exit the vehicle as I open the van door.

Sadie has his partner detained in the passenger-seat, his hands raised.

"Avery," I shout. "Are you okay?"

She delivers a low confirmation, her voice too faint. But she's talking. She's coherent. She could be in shock. The important thing is she's *alive.*

Once the guy who's wearing a blue jumpsuit is out and facing me, I lower my GLOCK and order, "Turn around and don't. Fucking. Move, you piece of shit."

I clamp a cuff around one of his wrists and secure the

other cuff to the side-view mirror before I hoist myself into the cab of the van. I unlatch the grate door. "Put your arm around me," I tell Avery. She does, clinging to my shoulders as I lift her out of the back.

"You saved me," she says against my chest.

My mouth turns down into a hard frown. "We're all here for you." I lock my arms around her and shuffle us into the driver-seat. I maneuver her off my lap with forced effort, desperate to keep her there—just feel her close to me and safe a minute longer. Then I climb down out of the van and look up into her face.

"You pulled off that hero thing pretty good." She smiles, but it's off. Her eyes glazed and pupils dilated.

"If I was any kind of hero," I say, "then you wouldn't be here in the first place." I grip her thigh once—one reassuring squeeze of my hand—before I turn to take my frustration out on the perp.

I uncuff him from the van and shove him against the front of the van, brining his hands behind his back. "You have the right to remain silent—"

The perp whirls on me and clips the side of my head with a direct punch.

Sonofabitch.

He's already taking off and running down the freeway within the seconds I recover. Fuck it. I give chase and tackle him.

As he struggles beneath me, I decide I no longer need my gun and lock it into my holster. This bastard is going to get a bit of old-school processing. And I'm damn sure going to enjoy it.

CHAPTER 11

THE DEPTHS

AVERY

I watch Sadie collar the guy in the passenger-seat. She yanks him out of the van, literally by his shirt collar, and I smile. She's so tiny, but somehow she manhandles him as if he's just a flea. She cuffs his wrists behind his back and commences reciting off his rights.

He's the one who wore the horror mask. I knew once the two men stripped the disguises away that I was not making it out alive. But I am. I'm here.

I shake my head to clear it, and my vision fills with tracers. My skin itches as the heat simmering beneath rises to the surface, demanding to be felt.

"Come on, Avery. You're safe," Sadie says.

I climb over to the passenger-seat, and she wraps an arm around my waist, offering support as I fumble my way out of the van. "Sadie…thanks," I say, my tongue feeling coated and heavy in my mouth.

As she helps me get my bearings, her eyebrows pull together. Her gaze drags over me, slow and curious. “What did they do to you? Avery, are you okay?”

I look into her face and smile. She’s so beautiful. I don’t think I’ve ever told her how lovely she is, with her long dark layers framing her jewel green eyes—eyes that see right down to the marrow of people.

I reach out and let my fingers skim her face, feeling her tantalizing, silky features grace the pads of my fingers. “Everything is fine,” I assure her, and I mean it. Right now, I could either fall blissfully asleep or stay awake forever. Both options sound equally appealing.

She curses under her breath, which makes my smile stretch hearing a foul word from her delicate lips. “Stay right here.”

Hauling her perp by his linked hands, she escorts him to the back of Quinn’s car, where she handcuffs him to the door and then locks him inside. She pulls something from the front seat before she’s back at my side. She slips her jacket over me, guiding my arms into the sleeves, then brings my face before hers.

Placing her hands on either side of my face, she tugs the sensitive skin down below my eyes, hers squinting as she performs an inspection. “You’ve been drugged. Do you know what they gave you?”

I nod. “Something that’s going to make me crawl out of my

skin here in about ten minutes," I answer honestly. I'm lucid—rational enough to understand the effects taking place—but it's as if I can't make myself care.

A frown pulls at Sadie's pretty mouth. "Okay. Let's go." She links my arm around her shoulder. We reach the back of the van, and I hear a loud groan followed by a curse.

Quinn has the other guy on the ground, his knee pressed into the middle of the man's shoulder blades. The guy—the one I stabbed with a pen—looses a string of swears into the gravel.

I've never seen Quinn get so...*physical* before. It does something to my insides. Watching him thrust his body weight on top of the guy stirs a primal and raw craving deep within me.

But true to Quinn's compulsive nature, he doesn't take it any further. He promptly stands, releasing the man and says, "Get up."

Beside me, Sadie sighs. "Quinn, we don't have time for this. Avery needs—"

The guy throws a punch at Quinn, shocking her silent.

"Okay," she says. "Do your thing."

My mouth pops open, but either the chemicals inside me or the fact that Quinn is shedding his coat, revealing straining muscles against his dress shirt, has me promptly biting my lip.

The guy spits dirt from his mouth, an angry scowl etched on his face. "I'm not through with you, pig."

Quinn leisurely strides to the back of the van, where he folds his coat neatly and lays it on the bumper. Then, rolling up his sleeves, Quinn returns to face the guy. He hauls back and lands a blow to the man's face. Right in his nose.

Blood covers the guy's face before he drops to the ground. Quinn drives his foot into the guy's stomach. The resounding choking is followed by the gasp of the man sucking all that dirt back into his mouth.

My chest explodes with heat.

Fiery currents zip and tangle, building into a roaring inferno deep within my core. I squeeze my thighs together, needing pressure to ease the ache.

As if in a trance, I start toward Quinn, but Sadie snags my sleeve. "Down, girl."

I have to settle for watching Quinn rough the guy up as he clamps handcuffs on his wrists and forces him to stand. It's a nice view, all that male testosterone cording his muscles tight… the way his slacks hang low on his hips…the determined look in his eyes.

Quinn gets the man to the car as we follow behind, and Sadie says, "Avery needs to get to a hospital. You take them in. I'll help her."

This gains Quinn's attention, and after he locks his perp inside the car, he nails me with a concerned look. It hits me like a wave, crashing into my being with a brutal force.

Desire to have him stare at me like that for hours…*days*…

thrums through me with vicious need. “I want Quinn,” I hear myself state.

His thick eyebrows hike up to his graying hairline, and it’s sexy as hell, the way this tough man nearly blushes. But Sadie’s the one to respond. “Not a good idea,” she says, starting to lead me away.

“You can’t take the bus,” Quinn says. “It has to be processed.”

Sadie doesn’t talk back, but the icy look she sends Quinn conveys more than words.

Squad cars pull up, sirens blaring, interrupting the impending standoff between them. Carson parks ahead of the two black and whites and quickly heads toward the van.

“Look,” Sadie says, lowering her voice for Quinn’s ears only. “There’s no time to radio in a bus. She needs a doctor *now*. Have Carson process the van. I’ll take his car.”

This isn’t right. It’s not what I want. What I *need*. I’m the one who designed the drug. I’m the only one who understands it. And the thought of having some young ER doctor fresh out of med school prod and probe me while I’m feeling like this… No way in hell.

I pull out of her grip and clasp onto Quinn’s strong arm.

Sadie blows out a long breath. “All right, then. I guess that settles it.”

I feel Quinn tense beneath my hold. “All right then—what?”

She nods to me. "Avery's safer with you, anyway. I'll take the perps in. I'll handle the paperwork and interrogation."

"No." Quinn's voice is a dark boom. It sends chills skittering over me. "Carson will handle the perps. You process the van."

She cuts a slitted glower his way. "What? Are you afraid I can't handle them?"

"That's, quite frankly, the very opposite of what frightens me, Bonds." He levels her with a cool look. My skin flames as something unsaid passes between them. "I know you can handle them just fine."

After a few tense seconds, Sadie's the one to relent. The wounded draw of her eyebrows reveals her surrender. "Just… Take care of her," she says, tossing Quinn's coat at him. Without another word, she heads off to meet Carson at the van.

As Quinn leads me toward the other car, I say, "You hurt her feelings."

His low groan isn't meant to be heard, but I can feel it rumble through him. "It's complicated."

I scoff. "That's an understatement."

He turns a sharp glare on me. "Whatever you think…" he trails off. "Forget it. We should be focused on getting you out of here. Were you…hurt?" he asks, a hesitant tone breaking through his concern.

I shake my head, wobbling a little as the ground rocks. "No, I wasn't. But that's complicated, too."

He stops abruptly and faces me. His hands cup my cheeks,

lifting my gaze to his, and my breath stutters. He angles my head back as he gives me his own, personal examination, his thumbs tracing the contours of my skin.

A shiver races through my body. I move into him, desiring his touch to brand me—to travel lower, exploring every inch of me. Slowly and meticulously. The way I know Quinn would.

I tremble as his rough fingers inspect my neck, the warmth of those hands that just issued a brutal punishment now feel tender—but I know the strength behind them.

A moan slips past my lips, and his hands fall away. "Don't stop," I whisper.

With a low growl, he scoops me into his arms and shouts an order at Carson. "Keys. Now."

I glimpse the confusion on Carson's face as we pass, but he does as instructed. He digs out his keys from his pocket and tosses them at Quinn. I snake them out of the air with a wicked smile.

"Taking me somewhere private, detective?" I ask.

His mouth presses into a hard line. "Yes. Your very own private hospital room."

He opens the car door with me still in his arms, then sets me in the passenger-seat. "We really need to stop this routine of you carrying me to cars, Quinn."

I'm surprised when a small smile lights his stern features. He rounds the car and slips into the driver-seat. As he buckles himself in, he says, "Are you hurt? In pain? Anything happen at all that—?" He stares at the wheel, a severe furrow creasing his forehead.

I lean toward him. "Nothing happened that you need to worry about. Maybe if this was the first time I was abducted…" I say with a shrug. "But by comparison? This was a pretty lame attempt on my life."

He doesn't seem to like my answer, and turns the key with more strength than necessary. Like he wants to tear the damn ignition off.

"Relax, Quinn." I rest my hand on his shoulder. The feel of hard muscle beneath my palm has my fingers working to ease his tension. His hand seizes mine, and he moves it to the console between us.

"Avery, if they hurt you…you can tell me." His eyes find mine then.

"I'm fine. I promise," I say, which is true. Any pain I might be in is dulled by the numbing effect of the drug. "In fact, all I need is my bed to sleep it off."

Pulling onto the road, he takes off in the direction that is the exact opposite of my house. "I'm not taking any chances," he says resolutely.

Then, against all logic trying to seep past the drug rushing my system, I do something so out of character that I would cringe at myself if I could. I actually hear myself whine. My body struggles against the seatbelt strap, the restraint intolerable. I cross my legs, tighten my thighs, applying enough pressure to sate the sudden onset of need.

Here it comes.

Panic laces my mind, and any rational thought evaporates. As the drug begins to crescendo, all inhibitions fly right out the window.

"Stop the car," I say, a frantic hitch in my voice.

"Avery…I can't."

"Stop. The. Car," I demand.

Quinn utters a curse as he pulls onto the side of the highway. He doesn't bother putting the car in Park as he gives me his full attention. "What's wrong?"

I lick my lips, my mouth desperate for liquid. "You can't take me to a hospital," I say, latching onto his hand. I squeeze as the pressure builds into a painful ache, and he lets me. I close my eyes for a few seconds until it ebbs. Then I release a slow breath. "Please, Quinn. I'm begging you. The thought of some doctor running tests…it's humiliating."

Confusion mars his face. "Then tell me, Avery. Make me understand."

I want to die. I want to curl into myself and just die. The realization of what I've created for those monstrous devils hits me with sickening force as a wave of ecstasy crashes over me.

"Oh, shit…" I breathe through a sharp spasm. Then I look into his eyes, anticipating judgment in his hazel gaze. But they only see me, reflecting none of the revulsion I feel. "I'm not sick, and I'm not overdosing. The cocktail I made? The aphrodisiac?" He nods his understanding. "Multiply that by a thousand, and that is what's coursing through my system right now."

A fierce gleam lights his eyes. A range of emotions—from sympathy to rage—wars within their depths. But I don't wait for the questions to come. I know he wants answers, but right now, I'm desperate to get somewhere safe and secluded.

"So please," I say, evoking as much commiseration in my voice as possible. "The last place I need to be is a hospital bed."

"Fuck," he bites out. He glances in the rearview mirror, then steers the car back onto the road. After he makes a U-turn in a strictly no U-turn lane, he says, "You're going to give me answers."

"I will," I say, pressing down into the seat to ease the mounting throb. "I'm going to help you get these bastards. But you need to get me through this first."

Another sharp curse fills the car, and the busted skin around Quinn's knuckles turns white as his grip tightens on the wheel.

CHAPTER 12

PURGATORY

QUINN

Sadie's not happy. Not one bit. But mother fuck, what can I do?

Avery has to know what's best. She's the brains of this operation. I have to trust that if she thought her life was in danger, she'd say so.

Trust.

That word batters my brain as I take the scolding from Sadie.

"After everything she's been through, Quinn. You need to man-up and make the right call *for* her."

Sadie's words make my jaw lock tight, my back teeth grinding down so hard I fear I'll crack a tooth. This job is going to put dentures in my head before I'm fifty. "Fucking hell. She's not a child. This is Avery we're talking about."

"I know," Sadie says.

"Then don't you think she knows what she's doing?"

A beat, then: "Okay. You're right."

Mother of mercy. I can't believe it. "Listen. I got Avery, so I need you focused on the perps. Wherever she was held, Avery said there was another woman there, and there could be more. Use Carson. Let him work them over, then you bring in the big guns. We need names and locations. Fire off all the charges—"

"Quinn, they've lawyered up. Right off the rip, they asked for some swanky lawyer named Maddox."

I squeeze my eyes closed. Mostly from hearing the name of the lawyer I've been investigating, but also to stop the sight of Avery undulating on the couch.

I turn toward the window. "I need you to get ahead of this. Maddox is dirty."

"Name me a lawyer who's not," she says.

We're on the same page there. "But he's connected to the first vic somehow. Theory is, she was a working girl. And if Maddox is representing our perps, he may know the whos and wheres. Get to him. Get those perps talking."

"You're asking me to be on this case?"

My back tenses. With a glance Avery's way, I frown. There's still too many unanswered questions—but the answers won't make a damn bit of difference at this point. Not when I need my partner working the angles that I can't.

"Everything you need is in my office. Get caught up as quickly as you can. And, Bonds," I say, my tone inflecting the seriousness of this request, "complete transparency. You do not make a move without me."

"I'll get Wexler to assemble a team. We'll locate this other woman and any others, Quinn," she says, and I know Sadie will do everything within her power for these women. "I'm on top of this. You just take care of Avery. I'll call when I have a lead."

I end the call, a weight of uncertainty dropping in my stomach. It's not that I don't trust Sadie to work the case, to find the answers. I've never doubted her when it comes to the job. This doubt is of a different beast—one that worries what she'll do with those answers after the fact.

And trust is everything between partners.

I tuck my thoughts away, getting my head back in the current predicament. Grabbing my forensic kit, I approach Avery, feeling as if I'm about to perform an exorcism rather than a forensic examination. "If you're not going in, then we have to collect evidence here."

For my sake, she stops grinding against the couch. "I can do it myself."

"You're under the influence of a drug." I kneel before her and open the kit. "You know how this works. Lawyers will have a field day tearing you down, getting any evidence thrown out." I'm extra cautious now; making sure any and all trace is collected right. Maddox is notorious for getting his clients off on bullshit technicalities. "So you have to tell me, Avery. If there's anywhere personal we need to examine—"

"There's not." She lifts her chin high, resolute.

I exhale my relief, a physical weight being removed from my chest.

Avery slips out of Sadie's jacket and lays it on the back of the couch. "My hair," she says, pointing to her head. "One of them may've scratched me. And my nails. Possible blood or epithelial cells." At my wary expression, she adds, "I stuck one of them with a pen."

Although it's absolutely inappropriate, this brings a smile to my face.

"What?" She balks at my reaction. "I wasn't going down without a fight. Not this time."

"Not any time." I pull on a pair of gloves and hold my hands out to her. She slides her palms against mine, and our eyes meet. A question lingers in hers. "You've never been anything but a fighter, Aves. I'm glad you got a piece of him. It will help."

I'm as gentle as possible while I scrape her nails. Moving on to gathering any trace from her scalp, I use a strip of tape to lift evidence. She shivers as I comb my fingers through her hair.

A pretty blush rises to her cheeks. "My scalp is extra sensitive."

These examinations aren't easy for anyone. And considering Avery is nearly crawling out of her skin, I'm impressed—and admittedly, relieved—that she remains still during the grueling process.

When I begin to explore her body with the miniature UV light, she arches her back, her breathing intensifying. *Exam over.* "I think you can handle the rest." I hand her the light, then pack up the Heme Stix.

"But I thought you said—"

"I know what I said." And damn, I've already strayed so far outside the lines of my own rulebook, at this point, what difference does it make? But that festering guilt still eats at me—the compulsion to *try* to do this by the book.

I don't even know who's rules I'm following anymore.

Setting the lamp down, Avery lies back on the couch. The restraint it took to keep composed during the examination shows. She trembles from that exertion. "I think you covered it," she says. "They were meticulous. We'll be lucky to get anything."

Taking a seat on the chair opposite her, I prop my elbows on my knees.

"You should let me doctor your knuckles," she says.

"They're fine."

Her intimate stare unnerves me. "Did you do that during the fight?"

I shake my head. "No. Before."

Through the haze of drugs, her eyes sharpen on me, but I'm relieved when she lets it drop at that. "Do you know them?" I ask, getting back on the topic of her. "Did you recognize them from anywhere?"

Her breathing is labored, her chest rising and falling heavily with each gasp for air. Sweat beads across her forehead, dampening her light hair. According to Avery, her desire to experience pleasure is so demanding it's physically painful. Her agony is unbearable to watch.

She attempts to shake her head against the pillow. "They didn't act or talk like the people I've dealt with before. I don't think these men have anything to do with my contacts on the darknet." Her eyes close for a brief moment as a sudden spasm hits. My frown deepens. "But you can check it out yourself," she adds when it passes.

She gives me the password to her laptop and rattles off some other screen names and access codes. I jot it all down in my notepad and then stand to get started, relieved to have something constructive to do. Despite my limited input on the case while here, I should still be able to investigate her darknet connections.

Another wave assaults her, and I come to a stop. "Is there anything I can do?"

Her brown eyes snap to mine. "You shouldn't ask that."

I force down the knot in my throat as her hungry gaze devours me. A lesser man would wilt under that gaze—would surrender to the temptation. And god, but Avery is tempting.

I clear my throat, avert my eyes to the floor. "What I mean is, if you explain how the drug works, maybe I can—"

She laughs. "Still detecting, detective? You want to know just what is being unleashed out there? What these fiends made me create…a drug that, as we speak—" she shifts to get more comfortable "—could be spreading out there right now?"

I huff my aggravation. "Yeah. Something like that. I have a responsibility to report it and take action to get it off the streets. Especially to keep it out of the hands of rapists."

She nods weakly. "That's the only logical conclusion, isn't it?" Her eyes spear me. "That I've designed a drug which will be used by men so wretched…so vile…they want to cause physical pain to a woman until she succumbs to her desires." She chokes back a cough, then pulls air into her heaving lungs. I'm moving toward her, but she holds up a hand. "Please don't. The last thing I deserve is sympathy. I've created the ultimate date rape drug, Quinn. And what's more terrifying…? I can't even fathom the full evil this drug can achieve."

It takes all my strength not to go to her. She's not just suffering the effects of the drug; she's punishing herself. And when she buckles over from the pain, it's more than I can stand.

I toss my notepad aside and yank off my coat as I rush toward her kitchen. Rolling up my sleeves, I locate a washcloth and run it under the tap. I wrap a few ice cubes in the cloth, my focus clear. The case can wait.

As I enter the living room, I don't give Avery a second to argue. I sit down beside her and pull her against my chest. "Lay your head back," I say, taking note of the fierce tremble in her body.

She's on fire. Her skin flush, her clothes damp from sweat. Even as she does what I ask, laying her back against my chest, I can feel her hesitancy. I stretch out my legs on either side of her and smooth her hair away from her face, then lay the cool cloth along her forehead.

"Just try to relax," I say. "You don't deserve this punishment, Aves. You didn't set out with this outcome in mind. Some very fucked up people used you."

Her chest rises as she sucks in a sharp breath, struggling to suppress a ripple of pain. "They knew they could, Quinn. They knew they could use me."

I brush her hair away from her neck, trying to alleviate the heat blanketing her. "I once worked a case where a stalker found his victims online. It was way above my head. Somehow, he was using programs he coded to locate these women by their search history. Certain keywords…sites they visited… the clues were in the metadata. I was just a regular detective, hunting a ghost on the Internet."

"Did you find him?" she asks, and I can hear the throaty pleading in her voice. She's building again. My jaw clenches as she wriggles to get some relief.

"Yeah, I did," I say, working through my own brand of punishment. "I had to learn a lot of shit that I never cared too much about before. Stuff I never thought would do me any good out in the field. That was what the techs were for, right?

But we caught him in the end. Set up a whole operation to lure him out of cyberspace and I made the collar."

"That's a nice story, Quinn. But what does it have to do with what I've done? With what we're facing?"

"That's what I'm going to figure out," I assure her.

We believe the killings started with the first dead pro, but what if she wasn't the first? What if there are other vics outside of the city who suffered a similar fate? Avery didn't give these bastards the idea for the drug; they were already in pursuit of it. Once I get the techs on the right trail, I'm sure we'll discover a connection. I'm almost damn certain this goes deeper than some new designer drug to sell over the black market.

Unfortunately, Avery was hunting a cure for her own personal dilemma in the wrong neck of cyberspace. It snagged the attention of the wrong people. That's where they found her, and that's where I'm going to use their own resources against them.

"Quinn…"

Avery's desperate tone breaks through my heavy thoughts.

I tug her more securely against my chest. "Honestly, Avery. What will make this better? There has to be something—"

"Touch me."

My eyes close against the onslaught of arousing thoughts her breathy words elicit. I bite out a curse. "Not happening, Aves. Not like this." I wrap my arms around her, offering her as much comfort as I can, but my hands stay locked in tight fists.

Not even a pinky allowed to roam.

Her body racks with shivers. "It's the only way. I have to relieve the pressure. Every time it mounts, the pain gets worse. If I don't…" she trails off, but her unuttered words ring clear. If she doesn't come—if she doesn't grant her body the release it needs—this torture will continue, becoming unbearable.

I suck in a deep breath past the blazing ache in my chest. "Will once even be enough?"

"I don't know," she answers truthfully. "And god, this is so humiliating."

"It's just me, Aves. There's nothing to be ashamed of. We're two grown-ass adults. We can handle this. Here—" I remove the cloth from her forehead and set it on the back of the couch. Enforcing my own speech, I keep my hands steady as I unbutton the top of her blouse, letting her body breathe. "Do whatever you need to get through this. I'm here. Moral support."

This makes her laugh, and I love the sound of it. Relief cuts through the tension. "Quinn, you're the epitome of moral." She takes my lead, undoing the rest of the buttons.

I bite back a groan as her lacy black bra makes an appearance, the sexy swell of her breasts capturing my attention. I should look away. That's the *moral* thing to do, but I'm obviously a glutton for punishment myself.

My eyes trace the beautiful curves of her tits as she runs her hands over them. Then, because I'm not in enough torment, she arches up and unfastens the clasp, setting herself completely free. My cock takes this opportune moment to go fully erect, and when she pushes back against me, the greedy shit indulges in the feel of her ass.

Control. I'm in control. I mentally recite this mantra as I forcefully tear my gaze away from her breasts, which are now on full display. Seeing her peaked nipples, pink and soft—Jesus Christ. I've never envisioned Avery naked before—and I'm glad. It would've been a disservice.

She's fucking breathtaking.

Her hands move lower only to halt at her belly button, and I stop breathing. "Undo my skirt," she says, her breathy request about sending me over the edge.

Hell no. I lock my hands at my sides. "Aves…don't ask me—"

"Please," she breathes out. "I just need the stimulation. I'll do all the work."

Fucking hell. I crick my neck, working out the gathering tension. But there's nothing to be done for the poor bastard in my pants. I'm already engorged and throbbing, and every subtle move Avery makes on top of me is a torturous tease to the sad fucker.

But this isn't about me. This is about the woman in my arms, getting her through the pain, and I'm man enough to do that. At least, I damn well hope I am.

With a resigned groan, I flex my fingers, accepting my

duty. I grip the button and give it a firm tug. It comes undone easily, and Avery bucks against me, arching her back and digging her ass into my groin.

My fingers nearly tear through the edges of the cushions as a jolt travels the length of my shaft. Only allowing myself a small thrust of the hips, I lift up; just enough to offset the overpowering need to bury myself inside her.

There's just not enough time to recover. As she assured, Avery does the rest. I watch, paralyzed, as she pushes her skirt down, wriggling it all the way off her legs and kicking it to the floor. Her hands wander over her thighs as she brings her knees up and parts her legs.

Punch myself out—that's my only option. Because there's no damn way I'm going to survive this.

She's going to fucking wreck me.

And as she tentatively roams her fingers over her lacy underwear, I all but lose my shit. She starts to push those down, too—and I grab her wrist.

"Those stay on," I say, my tone gruff, commanding.

She must hear the desperation breaking into my voice, because her movements halt. The elastic band snaps her hip as she releases it, then she gracefully slips her fingers under the lace. Her sensual moan nearly unravels the last of my control.

As her hand expertly works beneath her underwear, I swear it's the most erotic thing I've ever experienced. She thrusts her hips as she speeds her pace, meeting her need with timed perfection.

I've become entranced by some kind of morbid fixation, where watching her get herself off becomes as necessary as taking my next breath. I'm a needy, greedy fuck, and I'm surely going to hell for this.

"More stimulation," she begs. "I can't…get there. It's too much." She lifts her hips, over and over, each time coming down harder on my cock. I know she feels the thick ridge of it digging into her backside, but hell, I can't help myself.

I spear my fingers into my hair, losing all sense of control. "Avery, don't ask me this. I won't do anything that either of us will regret tomorrow. You can do this, Aves. Just relax."

Her whine pierces my chest, and I'm right there with her. My damn cock aches so badly…if she continues to grind against me, I'll fucking blow in my pants.

"Just a little more," she says, her voice a sexy rasp. "Play with my tits."

Holy fuck. That dirty talk coming from Avery's sweet mouth is my undoing. My cock jumps, and I have to push back in order to keep from clutching her hips to me.

Jesus Christ, I know I'll pay for this—but I reach for the ice-wrapped cloth and unravel it just the same, letting the cubes fall into my hand. As she arches her back, working her fingers deeper inside, I rest the tip of a cube to her nipple.

She gasps, undulating her hips hard and effectively bouncing her tits, getting the friction she craves from the ice.

With measured breaths, I slowly swirl the cube around her nipple. I'm so fucking hard I'm going to have blue balls for a week.

"More," she demands.

I switch hands, bringing the ice to her other nipple and applying more pressure, rubbing the perfectly peaked bud until she cries out. I drop the ice. "Shit."

"Quinn," she pants my name. "Stop fucking around and give me what I need, or this is going to take all night."

"You're not making this easy," I say, then bite my tongue. "Sorry. Not your fault. I'm just trying to respect you through this."

She releases an anxious laugh. "Always a saint. Even when a girl is begging for it."

My brow furrows. There's no reasoning with her. Not right now. But later, when she comes down, she'll probably hate my fucking guts for this. I ring out the cloth and place it over her chest, giving myself some kind of a barrier, at least.

Then, sending the last of my inhibitions to hell, I take her tits in my hands. She arcs into me as I caress her, and I hate myself but god—her breasts feel so damn good. Even through the infuriating rag, they're damn perfect. Heavy and full, with her silky nipples pebbling against the wet cloth. Right under my touch.

She relaxes again, her hand working eagerly beneath her underwear to get her there, while I rub my thumbs over her nipples, offering her as much stimulation as I can without losing my mind.

Only it's too damn late for that.

Right here, right this second, everything changes. That wall that keeps me safely guarded comes crashing down, and I'll never be able to desire another woman the way I desire Avery right now.

The want will kill me.

Just as I begin to crack, my sanity past the brink, Avery releases a sexy moan, her body trembling. Her thighs spread wide as she rolls her hips higher, her pussy thrusting eagerly as she breaks against her hand.

The sight of her has me pinching her nipples, just as desperate to feel her relief crash into me. I'm too close. My balls tighten, my cock ramrod straight and pulsing, but I rein it in. A growl rips loose as I clutch her tits, watching her milk the rest of her orgasm.

She falls limp against me, her hand sliding free of her underwear, and all I can think about is tasting those slick fingers. *Shit.* Not letting her get too comfortable, I say, "Avery, roll over."

Her body is spent. She groans but allows me to roll her onto her side. I jump off the couch with a harsh curse at my aching balls. I push at my rock-hard erection as I locate her bathroom.

Then I lock myself the fuck inside.

Bracing my hands on the marble counter, I heave deep breaths. I can't look at myself in the mirror. *Fucking saint*. She has no idea.

I flip the tap on and splash my face with cold water, thinking about grabbing some more ice to pack against my throbbing dick. Just the thought of lowering my zipper is too tempting, though. If I unleash myself now, I'll wear my cock out.

And there won't be any forgiving myself for jerking off to Avery's pain. Hot as hell…but I won't be that sick fuck.

Inhaling deeply, I can still smell her scent all over me. I tear my shirt off and press my back against the cool paneling of the door, praying like hell she's sated when I leave this room. As much as I want to help her, I won't be able to endure that torture again.

I do the only thing I can: I envision the bastards who did this to her, mentally putting my fist through their faces, and that swift bite of anger checks me.

When I'm composed enough to enter the living room, I almost collapse from relief. Avery's eyes are closed, and though she's suffering a fitful sleep, she's out. I settle on the floor near her, so I can listen to her shallow breathing. Making sure she stays safe through the night.

CHAPTER 13

SURRENDER

AVERY

The piercing shriek of the kettle assaults my head. I trip over my feet on my way to flip off the stove burner. After I move the kettle aside, I bury my temples against my palms, resting my elbows on the counter for support.

A hangover I can deal with. But this is a whole other level of day after dejection.

I plop a green tea bag into my cup and pour steaming water over it. Then I think better and make a second cup. I owe Quinn a hell of a lot more than a stupid cup of tea, but it's a start.

I feel his heady presence before I turn to see him standing in the entryway of the kitchen.

Our eyes lock, silence stretching out between us like a gulf. And I should feel desperate to fill it, but a strange comfort settles over me that he's still here. That he didn't fling himself out the door at the first ray of light.

His white dress shirt hangs open, black tie left undone, matching the unkempt look of his unruly hair. Which is the first time I can say I've ever seen Quinn out of sorts. My gaze roams lower to the tattooed words peeking from beneath his unbuttoned shirt. A quote covers the upper-right side of his chest. I first noticed it when I saw him stretched out on the floor this morning, but I still can't make out the words clearly.

"Tea?" I offer lamely.

His crooked smile sparks a flutter in my stomach. "Have anything stronger, like coffee?"

I shake my head. "Not in this house."

He cocks his hip against the counter, crosses his arms. "Tea is fine."

Turning my attention to the cups, I keep busy with adding honey, slicing lemons… "Thank you for being there for me yesterday." I add a slice of lemon to each cup and bob the tea bags. "And for not taking me to the hospital. I know it was asking a lot, and totally against protocol, but—" I face him, needing to look into his eyes, no matter what I find there. "It might not seem like it, but it was the right thing to do."

I wish I could read his mind. Know exactly what the slight furrow of his brow means, the serious, hard stare of his hazel eyes. When he breaks the intense stare off, it's to reach up and feel the scruff along his jaw.

"It might've been the right thing for you, but it was most definitely not the right thing for *me*," he says.

His words pierce my heart. "Oh," is my pathetic response.

Quinn's mouth hardens into a line. "I can't ever do that again, Avery."

Averting my gaze, I stare at my bare feet. My legs that I shamefully forgot to cover up and my dumb T-shirt that just barely hides my ass. After yesterday, I didn't feel the need to hide, or for any stupid pretenses. Obviously, I made a huge error in judgment.

"I should go get dressed. Your tea's on the counter."

I attempt to rush past him, but he clasps my arm and pulls me to a stop. I wince at the sudden stab of pain in my shoulder.

The mortified look on Quinn's face steals my breath. "It's not you," I rush out before he thinks the worst of himself. "My shoulder was hurt…yesterday."

His features relax, but just as quickly, his eyebrows draw together in concern. "I thought you said you weren't hurt?"

"I wasn't. Not really. But it's not as if they handled me like a delicate flower petal."

He scrubs his hands down his face, releasing a groan. Then he goes to touch my shoulder, and I step back.

"It's fine," I assure him. "Hot water will help."

Before I'm successfully out of the room, he says, "You do understand why?" I turn toward him. "Why that was so hard for me?"

A whole list of reasons quickly formulates. His feelings for Sadie. Getting involved with a colleague never ending well. Ruining a friendship.

But the one thing that sticks out—despite all my effort to suppress it—and coils my stomach in tight knots, is the one thing I know Quinn is adamant about.

Never get involved with a victim.

And regardless if he didn't see me as one before, that's exactly what I was to him yesterday.

I move closer, my embarrassment receding now that my anger mounts. "I get it, Quinn. I appreciate what must've been a difficult situation for you, and I'm sorry that it was me who put you in it." I swallow down the burn of resentment. "Don't worry, though. It won't happen again. I know the rules on victims, and I know that here, with me, is the last place you want to be."

That furrow in his brow deepens. "What the hell are you talking about, woman?"

My shock must be apparent. I shake my head in fast jerks, blinking hard to fight back the stupid, angry tears. "You claim you don't see me as a victim, and you put out all these mixed signals that I thought I was *finally* deciphering. But yesterday... Yesterday you could barely stand to touch me. It's almost as if the very thought of it was physically painful for you. I don't know if it's because it's me...or if the victim in me just disgusts you—"

Quinn moves so quickly that, before my last word is even voiced, his hand is in my hair and gripping me to him, his lips on mine.

The impact of his kiss rocks into me and I moan, unable to repress the sudden intensity of feeling his lips crushing mine. His other hand fists my shirt, then both are suddenly clutching my waist and lifting me off the floor.

I lock my arms around his neck as he hauls me across the kitchen. The counter where our cups tumble over, his destination. Then his hands are seeking my thighs, pushing the barrier of my shirt away, his mouth never letting up. Our breathing becomes ragged and desperate as we try to claim oxygen without losing each other.

When he does break the kiss, it's to capture my neck. His hungry kisses and branding nips send me spiraling, and I link my legs around his hips, needing him closer.

He pulls back. "Does this feel like I don't want you?"

My chest rises with my leaden breaths. I shake my head. "Why now?"

He groans. "Because now you're Avery. Not drugged, not on some chemical to fuck with your senses. And if you can't feel how badly I crave you—every fucking sexy bit of you—and if you don't get that I've never seen you as a victim, not once..." he trails off, his gaze becoming heated. "Fuck, Avery. I just need you."

"Touch me," I say, the only response I can give him.

He doesn't hold back. Not this time. Quinn consumes my senses; his masculine scent of cologne and leather, his rough hands adding friction to all the right places. And unlike before, when he barely allowed himself near me, he now ravishes me with a punishing voracity meant to tear down all obstacles.

As his mouth caresses my skin, his tongue and lips massaging the ache in my shoulder away, my hand subconsciously goes to my lips. Concealing the scar.

Quinn sharply changes course. His hand sinks into my hair, his thumb tilts my chin up, angling my face toward his. His other hand encircles my wrist, removing the barrier to my mouth.

"A force of habit…" I falter.

His gaze lingers on my lips as he moves in, sealing his mouth over mine and enveloping me in a sensual kiss. Then, he whispers, "Every. Fucking. Sexy. Bit of you"—his eyes ensnare mine—"is just as beautiful as the next part. You're beautiful, Avery. Even your scars are beautiful to me."

Then his teeth nip at my lip, tugging it into his mouth before he pulls me into a devastating kiss that shatters me.

I'm lit with a blazing heat as his hand finds its way between my thighs. With a swift, expert move, he tugs the lacy fabric aside, his fingers seeking me without hesitation. His back tenses underneath my hands as he swirls the pads of his fingers deeper. Cool air nips at my core, proof of my arousal.

"Christ, you're so wet," he whispers harshly against my

ear, and I can't help the smile stealing over my face. I'm wet—without any need of an aid.

I ache all over, completely insatiable. And when he pushes inside, filling me with two of his fingers and leaving them there…I tremble against him. "Oh, god, please move. I want to feel you inside me, Quinn."

His rough growl heightens my need, and as he gives in, sliding his fingers deeper and with more force, all I can taste and sense is him.

I want to dissect this feeling—to try to understand how it's Quinn that shreds my defenses. How with every other man—even with my cocktail—I have to power through the fear, block out the encroaching shadows.

But I can't stop my mind from spinning long enough to unravel the meaning. Quinn tastes like pleasure and sin and longing. Such a powerful combination of emotions that steal my reasoning…but it's as if I've always been aware of them. Just hovering on the edge of the both of us, waiting to be recognized. Like I've been denying myself a right to this feeling all of my life.

And now that it's unleashed, ripping us both open at the seams, I dread the loss of it.

I arch into him, unable to control myself as he works me closer, my walls clamping down around his fingers and my body begging for more.

He nips at my ear, ratcheting up my desire. "I should've

taken your pain yesterday, Aves," he whispers. "I should've tasted your sweet pussy until you came in my mouth…and the only thing you knew was pleasure and how badly I wanted you."

His words caress me, and as I build toward a climax, desperate to push past any banked uncertainty, I cling to his shoulders. He drops down and takes a nipple into his mouth, his hot tongue tasting me through my shirt, his teeth firing a sharp spike of need right through me.

"That's it," he assures. "Let me feel you come… I need to taste you."

He dips lower, leaving me panting and aching, but soon his mouth—that mouth I have never heard utter such sexy things—takes me completely, finishing me off. His tongue swirls fast and needy over my clit, tipping me over the edge, as his fingers bring on a deep and consuming orgasm.

He pushes one of my knees up, spreading my legs wider as he devours me, my core pulsing against his thrusts. Then he meets me there. His mouth swallows my moan with a hungry kiss, taking the rest for himself.

When my breathing calms, he slows the kiss and pulls away. His eyes fervently holding mine, he reaches down and unclips his phone. "Stay right here…" he says. "I have to return this call."

"I didn't even hear it ring," I manage to say around the receding aftershocks still thrumming through my body.

He crooks a wicked smile. "That does a guy's ego good, but it's on vibrate."

This side of Quinn…a girl could get used to. But just like that, Quinn is all business, his cop persona slipping into place like the gun he holsters to his shoulder harness.

He makes his call, getting updates from a tech on a recent search, and I can't help but eavesdrop. This concerns me, too, and no matter how badly Quinn might want to shelter me, I have more knowledge than he can imagine.

That thought dampens the moment, knowing he's completely unaware of my true abductor's identity, and has no idea that I'm connected to Wells' death, or how the men who took me yesterday somehow know how deeply my level of involvement goes.

I haven't even had time to process the reality of it all. Or what the hell it could all mean. But I do know that whatever is happening between me and Quinn changes things. The slight guilt I felt before in keeping Quinn in the dark has just multiplied by infinity.

Before yesterday, it was a necessity for Sadie and I to keep Quinn out of the know. I agree with her, that Quinn isn't built for secrets. That he wouldn't be able to shoulder our—*my*—guilt, trying to exist in a realm somewhere between his black and white belief system.

It would break him.

This much I do comprehend, but it still doesn't change

the fact that he's possibly the only one besides Sadie who can connect all the puzzle pieces. There's only one choice to make, really. As I'm even thinking this, watching Quinn pace the living room, I've already made it.

It's what grownups do. It's what responsible medical examiners do. We face our consequences, even when those consequences suddenly take on new meaning we never fathomed. How could I have known I'd find this…whatever the hell it is…with Quinn? And now, the chance of losing his respect and this connection to him is more terrifying than facing a prison sentence.

Oh, there's definitely that, too…but just how much punishment would he feel I deserve? How much do *I* feel is enough? Retroactively speaking, what I suffered at the hands of Wells should count toward that sentence. I believe I bore more than any future punishment could hold for me—but the law doesn't work like that.

Quinn doesn't work like that.

Timing is everything, however. And there's a selfish part of me that wants to hold on to this moment just a while longer—just to feel what it's like to be with Quinn, no blurred lines between us.

Too bad we didn't figure this out before my abduction. Before I was so irrevocably changed. At one time, I think I was the perfect girl for Quinn. Maybe that's still what he sees in me… But he won't see that anymore once the truth comes out.

Just how selfish am I? Right now, selfish enough to grab ahold of Quinn the second he ends the call. Push him against the wall and kiss him, tasting myself still lingering on his lips.

"My turn," I whisper against his mouth.

His strong hands capture my shoulders, holding me too far away. "Avery, you don't have to—"

"I know," I say, raising an eyebrow. "This is absolute *want*."

He sighs, but I can see and *feel* his resolve weakening. "That sketch you sent? The one of the partial brand on the first vic? There's been a hit. About fifty miles from here, a prostitute was found dead, abandoned in a Dumpster. Sound familiar?"

"Quinn—"

"Because of her profession, there was no autopsy. A large amount of opioids were found in her system, so the coroner recorded COD as a drug overdose."

I clasp his hands, moving them down my body to rest at the small of my back, as I push up against him. Tenderly, I press a kiss to his neck, inhaling the scent of his woodsy cologne, and revel in the feel of him pulling me closer.

"I promise," I say. "I'll be right there with you. We'll figure it out. We'll stop the bad guys, and we'll save lives. I just don't want this moment to end so soon—I just want us to stay here for a little bit longer." I bite his ear, loving the way he grabs my ass, grinding his cock against my belly. "Because when we leave through that door, we might not get it back for a while."

Or ever…

That thought pangs my chest and I squeeze my eyes closed, savoring Quinn's strong hands holding me.

I ease my palms along his chest, sinking my hands beneath the leather harness and sliding it off his shoulders. As I push the leather straps down his arms, the feel of his muscles cording tight beneath my touch elicits a thrill inside me.

He catches the strap before the harness hits the floor and dutifully sets it on the shelf. "What are you doing to me?"

"This," I whisper, gently tugging his black tie from his neck. I wrap it around my hand as it comes free of his collar. "Put your hands behind your back, detective."

A cautious expression crosses his face before he follows through. "Cop clichés?"

I nod. "And a little incentive to help you relinquish your control." Keeping his tie in hand, I back up enough to pull my T-shirt over my head. The way his shameless gaze takes me in bolsters my next move.

I press up against his chest, my nipples pebbling at the friction, as I maneuver the tie behind his back and link his wrists together. "Now I know you can get free, but if you want me to keep going, then you have to be good and stay in your cuffs."

I pop onto my toes and taste his lips, sneaking in a little bite as I undo his belt.

I wrap my fingers around him, and he releases a sharp hiss. "Jesus…I'm not going to make it."

Against my better judgment, I let a laugh slip. His severe frown cuts through me. "Quinn, like you keep saying to me, just relax." Then I give him a wink before I drop to my knees, pulling his pants and boxers down with me.

The fact that I'm staring at Quinn's cock should feel surreal. And it does, but at the same time, I can't deny that I've never been this thrilled before. Rumors circulate around the precinct, and I've heard things. Like how Quinn lost his marriage. How he hasn't dated since. And I've also sensed his attraction to Sadie.

So the thought of wiping his mind of every other woman and bringing him to his knees with my touch more than arouses me, and I'm taking him into my mouth with that very mission in mind.

He's rock hard as I wrap my hand around him, his veins swollen, his shaft hot and thick. A salty taste of pre-cum hits my tongue, and I swirl it around the soft tip. He rocks his hips into me, and I let him fuck my mouth, taking him in deep.

"Christ, Avery..."

Hearing my name groaned out in Quinn's husky way has me wet and aching. I use a hand to brace his backside, sucking him in deeper, suddenly unable to get enough.

The tense muscles in his ass, the way he pulls against the restraint of the necktie...has me seeking his face. My gaze travels up to capture his stare. My breathing intensifies as I watch his expression shift from yearning to ravenous. The hard gleam in his eyes conveys just how badly he wants this—wants *me*.

It's more than empowering; it's liberating.

I don't feel vile or dirty. I don't try to disappear into some sheltered space of my mind, waiting for the moment when I feel normal again. That realization beckons me on, giving Quinn every last bit of me, taking him with me past the point of ecstasy.

And soon he's there, the rumble of his growl-like groan thrumming through me as he thrusts his cock toward the back of my throat. He releases into my mouth, and I don't pull away. I clasp his balls and bear the gagging reflex as he comes.

His hand goes to my hair. His fingers grip a handful, and as he pulses against my tongue, I moan, letting the vibration of my voice take him over the edge.

He reaches down and hauls me to my feet, his mouth finding mine before any words are exchanged between us. With a blistering kiss that scorches my lips, Quinn grasps my face, holding me to him, his hard length still throbbing against my stomach.

"God, your mouth… I fucking want you so bad," he says, his gruff voice a satisfying friction against my skin. His eyes flit over my face, tracing my features as if he's trying to put together a clue. "How—?"

"Don't detective this to death," I say, stopping him before we both spiral down a wormhole of guilt. I don't want to go there…not yet. "Let's just…shower? Which is more than you should get for breaking out of your tie." I wink at him.

His lips twist into a smile, but the blaring ring of his phone steals it away.

He releases me, and I cross my arms over my chest, the chilly air now noticeable without his comforting body heat. I then scoop my shirt off the floor, realizing that a shower isn't happening as I listen to Quinn's angry barks into the phone.

Reality had to come crashing back at some point. And when he hangs up, his arms flexing with the tight grip he has on the phone, that reality is frighteningly real.

"Get dressed, and grab some extra clothes and things," he says, not facing me.

"Why? What's going on?"

Quinn yanks his shirt together and starts buttoning it, then turns around, his face devoid of any of the passion we just shared. "There's been an upset at the precinct. I can't leave you here. You're going with me. We'll figure out a security measure—"

"I'm not—"

"You are," he cuts me off. "You're in danger, Avery. For now, the only thing I can do to make sure you're safe is keep you close."

As he looks me over, his shoulders deflate. He moves before me and wraps his strong arms around my waist. Resting his lips against my forehead, he says, "I'm not good at this. But

I am good at my job, Aves. Let me protect you."

I nod against him. "I know. Okay." Which means that our little bubble has popped.

"Give me time…and once we catch whoever is responsible for hurting you—"

"Quinn," I say, putting my hand against his chest and inching away. "It's fine. Let's go get the bad guys."

CHAPTER 14

DELIVER US

QUINN

Finding the leak in the department should've been my top priority after closing out the last case. Although the bastard went silent after having nothing more than misdemeanors and traffic tickets to hand to the press, still, with the turmoil the serial killer case caused, it was only a matter of time before something like this happened.

The bullpen echoes with an annoying, scratchy feedback, the many flatscreens all tuned to the same news channel blaring a reporter's voice. Desks are abandoned, phones ring nonstop, and as Avery and I round the corner we come to a quick stop. A large group has congregated around one of the wall-mounted TVs.

"Come on," I say, taking Avery's hand. I lead her away from the crowd, circling back around toward my office.

I need her here to ensure her safety, but by the way her face just paled with panic, she's not ready to handle a flood of questions or give a statement. Besides, other than making sure she's protected, that's why she's with me—Avery's not giving her statement to anyone else so it can be leaked to the damn media.

Closing the door behind us, I flip the blinds down. Then turning toward my desk, I balk at seeing Sadie seated in my chair. "What are you doing here?"

I don't mean it to come out as asinine as it does, but as she's used to my bullshit, she just smirks. "You told me to catch up, remember? And I *was* getting further on your research until this happened." She turns the laptop screen toward us. "This is the second broadcast. Wexler is fuming." She glances between Avery and me. "And he's really pissed that Avery wasn't brought in right away."

I'm sure that's an understatement. The captain will have my badge before the end of the day. I dented up my car pretty good and ordered Sadie to shoot at a van in open traffic. And after everything that happened this morning…I won't even argue.

"But I was able to calm him down," she continues. "I told him that Avery needed to recover. He doesn't like it, but he's more focused on the recovery of other possible abductees." A faint smile breaks across her strained features. "I think I saved your badge. For now."

"Thanks," I say, knowing I owe Sadie more than that.

She shrugs. "What are partners for?"

My mind flashes back to the hospital the night of Avery's rescue, when I told Sadie something similar. "Were you able to get anything out of the perps?"

She shakes her head. "They're in holding. Can't touch them until after the bond hearing."

Fuck. "I'm sick of this red tape shit. And now any investigation into Maddox is going to be impeded."

"Not to mention how bad it will look going after a lawyer running for the DA's office," she says. "Wexler's going to order us to lay low until we find evidence on him that's not circumstantial. We don't have anything, Quinn."

"Hell," I scoff. "Even if he's not our guy, he's involved in this shit storm somehow."

As Sadie stands to embrace Avery, I give them privacy to talk amongst themselves and locate a statement report. Then, clearing my throat, I hand the paperwork to Sadie. "Do you think you can help walk her through it?"

She nods assuredly. "Of course."

As Avery and Sadie go over the events of yesterday, working out Avery's statement and hopefully finding some leads to open an investigation into Maddox, I hit a key on the laptop to play back the news report. Taking a seat at my desk, I turn up the volume.

"The cryptic instructions soliciting the abduction of one

of Arlington's lead pathologists went viral after it was leaked over the Internet this morning," the woman news anchor says. "Authorities have issued no statement, however, on the condition of Medical Examiner Avery Johnson, although our inside sources confirm she's alive and recovering."

"Inside sources," I mock.

This snags Sadie's attention and she looks at me. "Only someone in this department could've known, Quinn."

I hate that she's right.

"The leaked missive held detailed information on Johnson's whereabouts. Though dictated in a form of code, specialists have been able to decipher the signature"—the screen transitions to show the missive in question—"which has been identified as an emblematic signature for an underground crime ring known as the Alpha-Omega network."

"Shit." My adrenaline spikes as I recognize the design at the bottom of the letter. The same design branded on our vics. Jesus, these press assholes better not get ahold of our lead. If the media gets wind of other women captives, it will turn this investigation into a circus.

The anchor's face reappears on the screen. "Two suspects have been arrested and are being detained for further questioning in connection to Johnson's abduction. This was not the first time Johnson was targeted amid an ongoing criminal investigation, however." As the news anchor recounts Avery's captivity, I lower the volume, hoping to spare Avery the heartless recap of her own painful memories regurgitated over the Internet.

"The recent attack on Johnson follows closely behind two deaths which are currently under investigation," she continues, and both women move closer to the desk. "Could the deaths of Marcy Beloff and Lauren Carter, who were presumed dead due to suspicious circumstances, be tied to the Alpha-Omega network? And are the two suspects in question responsible for trying to silence the medical examiner who may have that answer? No further information has been—"

I kill the feed, my temper rising. Closing my eyes, I massage the sudden pain throbbing at my temples. "How the *fuck* does the media have an ID on the second vic before we do?"

"That signature," Avery says, her soft voice a soothing balm to my blistering thoughts. "It's almost identical to the brand on the vics. Quinn, in the lab yesterday, the men who took me forced me to change the COD reports on the victims to accidents. I was given the second vic's name to record. I'm not sure how it was leaked…but is this really connected to some crime organization? That just seems so…"

"Convoluted," Sadie supplies.

My irritation flares before I can rein it in. "Why didn't you mention the COD reports before?"

Avery's gaze narrows on me. "A lot has happened in the past twenty-four hours," she snaps, but I can hear the hurt behind her anger. "I'm sorry. It slipped my mind until now. I'll add it to my statement, of course."

I'm an asshole. I was busy getting my rocks off…and now I'm victim blaming? Fuck. "Sorry. I didn't mean for it to come out like that." I hold her gaze, trying to convey that I regret nothing that happened between us.

Sadie scans both our faces in turn, her eyebrow craned in question, but she sidelines her interrogation for now. I know it's coming later, though. Damn profilers.

Avery waves off my apology. "I know. It's fine. I'm high-strung, too." She exhales heavily and pushes her hands into her hair. "But now that I'm back, I need to get to my lab and straighten out those reports before the press tries to link me to some half-hatched conspiracy."

I pin her with a heated glare. "No. The lab's off-limits."

Crossing her arms over her chest, she matches my stare. "No offense, Quinn, but technically, you're not my boss."

I hear a muffled snort and glance at the source. Sadie covers a hand over her mouth, refocuses her attention on the statement.

A knock sounds at the door, saving me before I blurt something else asinine. Carson peeks his head inside.

Fucking hell. "Does no one have a job to do around here?"

"Sorry," Carson says. I wave him in, impatient. "But last time, I kind of got my ass chewed for this. Wanted to make sure you heard it straight from the source." He acknowledges Avery with a nod her way. "Welcome back."

"Thanks," she says. "I'm kind of tired of leaving."

Gritting my teeth, I bury my irritation with the intimate way in which he's staring at Avery. "Christ. What now, Carson?" I say, pulling his focus to me.

"Right." He sets his laptop on my desk right beside mine and taps the keyboard. The same news anchor comes alive on the screen. "Just watch," he says.

"Sources now tell us that the two victims have been positively tied to the Alpha-Omega crime ring. Both the deceased bore the branded emblem of what we now know is the Alpha's signature on their person." A close-up of the letter highlighting the design appears in the upper right corner of the screen.

"Fuck," I shout, and Avery flinches. I go to say something to reassure her, but Sadie points to the screen.

"Quinn, listen," she says.

"Are the recent murders and the attempted silencing of the ACPD medical examiner being kept from the public on purpose? Jeff Jackson is live now with the suspects' lawyer to answer our questions."

The backdrop alternates to a transmission of Maddox walking in front of the courthouse, the press holding microphones alongside him as they keep pace. His slick dark hair gleams in the sunlight, and though his mouth is set as grim as his clients' circumstance, there's a smile in his eyes. I already disliked this bastard before I ever laid eyes on him.

The reporters sling questions at Maddox, demanding to know if his clients murdered the victims; if the victims were prostitutes connected to a crime ring; if he's the acting attorney for the crime ring itself; if his clients attempted to kill the medical examiner working the case; if the ACPD is involved with a cover up; if Maddox knows who the Alpha in charge of the crime ring is. "No comment at this time," is his calm reply.

"With all this damning evidence, why haven't the local authorities confirmed the suspects in custody are indeed responsible?" the news anchor asks as the screen blinks to her. "With the city just suffering a tragic murdering spree, the public has a right to know if there's yet another serial murderer on the prowl. Do the police have the Alpha Killer in custody now, or is he still out there, branding his victims? Is there a new threat in Arlington, a powerful head of an underground organization that oversees the killing of women?"

I'm out of my seat and slamming the laptop closed, just stopping myself from throwing it across the room. "A department full of detectives and we can't find one goddamn leak?" I shout.

Sadie grabs the laptop, getting it out of my reach before I demolish it. "Department issued," she says in way of an explanation and hands it over to Carson. "Quinn, you know how the press work. They've used this Alpha-Omega scheme before to fan fires for ratings."

I heave a strenuous breath, my blood pressure rising. "But

who the hell served them up that bullshit on the brand being a signature? I want a team on that pronto. I want it discredited, but I also want to fucking find out what the hell it actually means."

Alpha Killer.

My jaw tightens, and I breathe through the restriction seizing my chest.

I scoop up the search report I requested yesterday, the one that shows a hit for the brand on a dead pro outside of the city. No mention of any fucking underground criminal network on the report. Which means we have nothing on it in the database, because it *doesn't* exist. It's a damn urban legend the press cooked up to increase ratings, just like Sadie said.

"Let him be a figment of the press's imagination," Sadie says, reading me like she always does. I look up. "The media can run circles around the Alpha Killer story. It will keep them busy and out of our way. They don't have the one key piece of evidence that matters." My office settles with a thick silence as that fact clicks into place.

I eye Carson, slitting my gaze. "Who all has had access to the M.E. reports?"

"Just us," he confirms. "With what happened to Avery... there hasn't been time for anyone to investigate the vics further."

But there has been. Because the press somehow got their leaked information from the doctored COD reports that had no mention of the drug. Avery's update on the cause of death was just simply overlooked. Accidents don't make for good news.

"Avery, I need for us to access your reports, and no one else outside of this team is permitted to see them."

She nods hesitantly. "All right, but for what it's worth, this doesn't seem like something one of ours would do. The leak, I mean. I know you can't really trust anyone..." Her voice lowers as she trails off. "But I can't believe that any one of my colleagues would throw me to the wolves like that."

After everything she's been through, no one would fault her for losing faith in the system. Shit, I wouldn't blame her for giving up on it entirely after what she just suffered. But hearing her contradict that assumption ignites some kind of fire in my chest.

It's a feeling I've been missing for a while.

Vindication.

I want it for Avery. And I want it for the ACPD.

"Are you wearing the same suit as yesterday?"

And like that, Sadie's keen observance knocks me right off my pedestal of justice.

Ignoring her outright, I point to the whiteboard. "We need to scour Maddox's list of high paying clients. Find out which ones enjoy extra curricular activities with working girls. Maddox has been with at least one of the vics. And this guy here—" I shuffle through the notes in my desk until I find what

I'm searching for. "Price Wells. He was a partner at Maddox's law firm before he was found dead. Didn't he end up on your slab, Avery?"

She pulls her bottom lip between her teeth, and I try hard not to think about how soft and tempting that mouth is. "He was…I mean, yes, he did. He was the first vic I autopsied after—"

Sadie takes ahold of her hand, offering her a comforting touch. I look away, feeling like a bastard for bringing it up now. It could've waited until she was better…settled.

"I'm not questioning your findings," I assure her, my gaze lowered to the COD report. "But I think we need to look deeper into this. Find out why so much shit is suddenly revolving around this law firm. Find out if Maddox or anyone else had a reason to want him dead."

"And this illusive crime ring?" Sadie says, steering my notice to the laptop screen.

I prop my hands over the stack of paperwork, giving it some thought. "It's bogus. We know that. There's never been one single conviction linked to it. But just to cover our ass, contact Agent Rollins."

A hint of shock registers on Sadie's face. "You want to bring in the FBI."

"No. Not bring them in, just feel them out. See if you get any kind of reading off of Rollins. Suss out whether he knows something." I scrub my hands down my face, already feeling the weight of this case burying me. "First, get to Maddox. If he's not our perp, then the perp might have ties to him and that firm. Either way, Maddox is dirty and I want his clients talking. Soon."

"All right. I'll follow that lead," Sadie says, then gives Avery a reassuring smile before she releases her hand.

"Take Carson with you." I catch Sadie's gaze, and it's there in her green eyes, that flicker of suspicion. But whether it's stemming from her or me, I'm not sure.

"Okay." She nods. "I guess the partner thing is on hold for a while."

A heavy silence chokes the air. I push back in my chair, gripping the armrests. "You're my partner, Bonds. But right now, I need to make sure Avery's protected. I know you can handle this, but with all the shit going down within the department, it's wise to have some backup with you."

She holds my gaze a moment longer, understanding passing between us. Then she releases a resigned sigh. "Got it. I'll take the rookie with me. No problem."

Carson steps forward. "You both know that I've been a detective now for—"

"You're still a rook," Sadie cuts him off. "And right now, you're a rook who's going to follow my lead with Maddox. He's not our typical person of interest. He knows the law, and he knows how to get around it." She eyes Carson with raised eyebrows. "We're clear?"

His mouth hardens into a line as he chews back a retort. He nods once.

I push away from my desk, going over the new facts as I head toward the whiteboard. I have no doubt Sadie can handle Maddox, and Carson, for that matter. I just hope she doesn't handle them too well.

Wiping the board clean, I say, "This is what we know, and these are the people we know it about." I jot down four names across the top of the board.

Ryland Maddox. Price Wells. Lewis Sellars and Markus Right—the two perps we wrangled down yesterday for Avery's kidnapping counting as one.

"Bonds and Carson are on Maddox. Get information on Wells while you're there. If Maddox is running for the DA's office, he knows he needs to work with us. Use that angle to get as much as you can without coming up against a warrant. He won't want the lives of these women on his hands. See if you can work any information out of him without giving away our lead."

I clear my throat, adjusting my stance. "Avery and I will work the two perps and the evidence angle that the press don't have." I make eye contact with both Sadie and Avery, relaying silently that no one mentions the drug. Not even to Carson.

"Someone is leaking like a damn faucet in this department," I add. "I want them flushed out. So anyone approaches you, anyone asks to get updates or access to the case, you report it to me."

"What about the other?" Carson pipes up.

"What other, Carson?" I ask, barely masking my frustration.

He moves farther back, tucking his laptop under his arm, as if I'm liable to hit him. With how today's going, that's wise.

"What about adding the Alpha Killer to the list?" he says, cringing after it's out there. "Look, I get that we hate monikers. I'm all about frowning on the moniker. But I think it's unwise to ignore the possibility altogether that there may be one top dog out there running the show. I mean, look at the idiots in holding," he says with an awkward chuckle. "No offense, Avery. I'm sorry. I can't imagine what you went through—"

"None taken," she says. "They are idiots."

Carson gives her a smile. "What I'm saying is, they don't seem capable of putting together an elaborate plan like breaking into the ACPD crime lab, stealing a bus, kidnapping a smart woman like Avery…all on their own. Not those two. They must've gotten their instructions from someone. Like that leaked missive on the news? Where did that come from? Who leaked it?"

I open my mouth to comment, but Avery intercepts his questions. "They did have help," she says, her eyes finding mine. "And he was intelligent. More than that, he was calm and in no hurry, completely in control, as if he felt he had nothing to fear."

I swallow the burning lump trying to strangle me. "Did you get a look at him?"

Her gaze shifts to the whiteboard, away from me. "No, I didn't. I don't think I'll ever forget his voice, though."

A pain barrels into my chest. I press my hand against it, then adjust my gun strap, attempting to conceal the move. I asked her over and over if she'd been hurt, and each time, she was quick to deny it. But then, she's been hurt before. Her tolerance for pain and suffering has increased. Maybe she even believes what she endured doesn't register compared to other hurts and scars inflicted upon her.

But the way she lowers her eyes now, the sullen inflection in her tone…I know this bastard *did* hurt her. And now, I'm going to make him pay for that.

I turn toward the board and do something I'd hate myself for any other day. With a tremor of rage in my hand, I write "Alpha Killer" in large print and circle it. "This fucker has a name. I want it."

CHAPTER 15

ALPHA

Wells was a loss. One of my best assets. You know that scene in Scarface, the one where Michelle Pfeiffer says, "Don't get high on your own supply." Ah! What a brilliant bitch. All criminals should be required to watch that movie before they're inducted into the fold.

I have my own preference for the order of rules. Don't sample your own product—lesson number one. Lesson number two: don't make a mess you can't clean up.

Wells had to be cleaned.

He sampled his own product, and he got messy.

Luckily, a pretty little profiler took care of the nasty task for me.

A man obsessed is a dangerous thing. You can't reason with him. He has no boundaries, no limitations. The whole world could be burning down around him and yet he'd only be conscious of his obsession.

Obsession makes you weak. And for that, Wells got what he deserved.

How I do miss his gifts, though. Wells knew quality. The gems he provided were never missed, always clean. Beauties, they were. Absolutely delectable.

They made me a lot of money.

And money…now that's what it's all about. Sex, drugs, power—all these things can be bought. Even your fucking, pitiful obsessions can be obtained with enough of it.

I stub out my cigarette on the dirty counter, disgusted. I hate mess. I despise filth. It sickens me almost as much as finding a rat in my presence. But here I am, cleaning up yet another mess. But if you want something done right… You know how it goes. No one gets to the top without getting their hands dirty every once in a while.

And I'm not afraid of work.

My once right-hand man is strung up in the middle of the room, his body stretched, limbs racked. He's soaked in his own sweat and piss. The stench of it rolls through the small space, souring the air.

I flick my hand, and two of my thugs lower him to the ground. Alex slumps over, gulping in the foul air, thinking the worst is over. That now, finally, his torture will end.

But death isn't coming to him so quickly. I invested much

of myself into Alex King. Reared him into my perfect protégé, and how does he repay me?

Red colors my vision.

I suppress my rage with a sigh of disappointment.

I do enjoy giving my rats a moment to catch their breath—to believe I might just spare them. Some have come to the conclusion that I've gone soft. I've seen the rebellion in their eyes, waiting for an opportune time to strike.

This will serve as a reminder to all.

Rule number three: If you're powerful enough, fuck the rules. Make your own.

Thumbing through my phone browser, I pull up a video and place the screen before Alex's face. His swollen eyes struggle to latch on to the images, but he can hear just fine.

"It wasn't me, boss," he slurs through busted lips, red-tinged spittle streaming down his chin. "I'm not a rat."

"Maybe you're not," I say, taking a lap around him. "But you did fail to bring me the lovely medical examiner. I'm almost inclined to believe you let those two imbeciles get caught on purpose."

He tries to shake his head, but only slumps over farther. *Pathetic.* "No, boss. Some cop cut me off. I promise, there wasn't anything I could do—"

One of the thugs punches him, effectively silencing his rambling.

I brush my hands down my Armani slacks as I squat

before him. I look him in his eyes. "I believe you."

For a second, his features convey relief. Until he notices the blade in my hand.

"But that doesn't change the fact that you failed me, and now the press have a direct order in their clutches." I *tsk*. "That is sloppy, Alex. How did they get it?"

"The van. It's the only logical place where I—" His eyes squeeze shut as he realizes his mistake. "It's the only place it could've been found," he finishes.

"Because you left it there."

He stammers out an excuse, and is greeted with another punch to the face.

I look down at the shiny blade, run it over my sleeve. Back and forth. "Do you know why the devil is so powerful?" I ask. His lips tremble, offering no reply. "Because the world doesn't believe he exists." Another effective quote that I enjoy. Kevin Spacey said it best: *The greatest trick the devil ever pulled was convincing the world he didn't exist*. Though technically, Spacey butchered an even greater quote from Baudelaire. Ah, semantics. The meaning is clear enough. It preaches to my heart.

I drive the blade into his stomach and slice straight up through his sternum.

His garbled cry catches in his throat as blood gurgles up, choking him off. I carve out a section of his chest, peeling the inked insignia from his bones.

"Take his skin," I order.

As I stand and fling the flesh away, I wipe my hands off on my handkerchief. Soon Alex does find his voice again. With each razorblade that splits his skin, with every yank of his flesh as it's stripped from his body, his wails fill the void above, his blood stains the floor.

My once right-hand man, now scorched earth beneath my feet.

No one will doubt me now.

I grab my phone off the floor and pause the video of the news broadcast. Her beautiful face fills the tiny screen, her deep brown eyes staring right into mine. Avery Johnson.

I pull Alex's gun from my belt, bring it close to my face. Inhale her scent that still clings to the barrel. At least Alex was persuasive in getting her to fulfill her purpose. And now I have a marketable drug for my clients. I just hate loose ends. They're messy.

"Donavan," I say, stealing my new right-hand man's attention away from his clean up. "How many novices do we have in transit?"

He looks up at the ceiling, actually counting out the number on both hands. A blinding rush of fury to stick my blade through his neck grips me.

"Seven, boss," he finally says.

"The media needs a serial killer," I say, walking toward the steel door. "So we'll give them one. If they're looking for *one* sadistic man, then they're not seeking the truth."

I throw the door open, and the muffled cries of frightened young women echo throughout the warehouse. Bound and gagged, they clamber together, crawling toward the back as if grouping themselves will save just one.

Looking over my suit, I decide it's already ruined. Blood soaks my sleeves; Alex's guts have made a disgrace of my shoes. I smile and raise my blade, pointing it at each girl in turn. "Eeny meeny miny moe, who will be the first ho to go."

As I said, I don't mind doing the work myself. It's good to get back to your roots every once in a while. Keeps you sharp. Keeps things in perspective.

The tip of my blade lands on a busty blonde. I grin, liking the idea of my fingers running through that hair, gripping a handful and yanking her head back. My blade slicing off her tits after I've fucked her pussy raw.

"Donavan. Get a direct line to the medical examiner." I wrench the girl free of the whores. "Time to send a message to Doctor Avery Johnson."

I float in a sea of limbo, lost but for the light of your voice, my destination. The haunted undertow of secrets drag me to the depths, drowning but for your saving touch, my anchor. ~Avery Johnson

Titles by
TRISHA WOLFE

Broken Bonds Series

With Visions of Red: Broken Bonds, Book One

With Visions of Red: Broken Bonds, Book Two

With Vision of Red: Broken Bonds, Book Three

With Ties that Bind: A Broken Bonds Novel, Book One

With Ties that Bind: A Broken Bonds Novel, Book Two

With Ties that Bind: A Broken Bonds Novel, Book Three

Derision: A Novel

Living Heartwood Novels

The Darkest Part: Living Heartwood (Book 1)

Losing Track: Living Heartwood (Book 2)

Fading Out: Living Heartwood (Book 3)

Darkly, Madly Series

Born, Darkly: Darkly, Madly Duet 1

Born, Madly: Darkly, Madly Duet 2

ACKNOWLEDGMENTS

Thank you to:

My amazingly talented critique partner and friend, P.T. Michelle, for reading so quickly, giving me the much needed pep talks and advice, wonderful notes, and for your friendship.

My super human beta readers, who read on the fly and offer so much encouragement, I could not write books without your brilliance. Honestly, you are my girls! Katrina Tinnon, Naomi Hopkins, Amy Bosica, Michell Casper, and Melissa Fisher. I really can't express how much you mean to me—just know that I couldn't do this without you. Thank you.

A special shout out to the girls who keep me sane in the Wolfe Club, where it's perfectly acceptable to be anything but ;) You girls are the best. You make me laugh, keep me motivated, and offer so much support, you have no idea. I adore every single one of you. And a special thank you to my girls in the group for helping me get this book in shape! Thank you!

My awesome assistant, Naomi Hopkins. I could not get through one book without your insightful input, girl. You go above and beyond an assistant's duties to help me sort through my chaotic life. Thank you for being a friend.

To my family. My son, Blue, who is my inspiration, thank you for being you. I love you. And my husband, Daniel, for your support and owning your title as "the husband" at every book event. I love you, too. To my parents, Debbie and Al, for the emotional support, chocolate, and unconditional love—I love you guys right back.

Najla Qamber of Najla Qamber Designs, thank you for so much for not just creating this stunning, take-my-breath-away cover, but for also just rocking so hard! You were so much fun to worth with; you took the stress right out of the very stressful task of series cover creation, and I cannot wait to work with you again on future projects. This cover is everything I envisioned and more.

A special acknowledgement to Damaris, thank you for being not only a wonderful friend, who's there when I just need to call someone, but also a huge support of my career. You mean so much to me.

There are many, oh, so many people who I have to thank, who have been right beside me during this journey, and who will continue to be there, but I know I can't thank everyone here, the list would go on and on! So just know that I love you dearly. You know who you are, and I wouldn't be here without your support. Thank you so much.

To my readers, you have no idea how much I value and love each and every one of you. If it wasn't for you, none of this could be possible. As cliché as that sounds, I mean it from the bottom of my heart; I adore you, and hope to always put out books that make you laugh, swoon, and cry.

I owe everything to God, thank you for everything.

ABOUT THE AUTHOR

From an early age, Trisha Wolfe dreamed up imaginary worlds and characters and was accused of talking to herself. Today, she lives in South Carolina with her family and writes full time, using her imaginary worlds as an excuse to continue talking to herself. Get updates on future releases and events at TrishaWolfe.com

Made in the USA
Columbia, SC
27 April 2023